Marked From Gold

Venus Grimm

Editor: Amrita Raza

ISBN:
979-8-218-42638-5

To those who feel like they are always on the run -
this will find you.
Keep pushing through.
- VG

CONTENTS

Crystal View News

Many more Deaths

Who else knows about Kindal Stewart?

A case that was closed fifteen years ago after Zira died of old age five years ago - Reopened

As a recap, Grandma Zira, savior of the town and grandmother of one beautiful girl, claimed to have a second grandson. These accusations had been investigated by police, but everyone seemed to have an alibi. Everyone except for her granddaughter Ziona, who was born mute. Her mother is restricting her from communications because she claims it is too "stressful." The mother of Ziona, Zira's known grandchild, claims that she never had twins. When investigating her house, the police found masculine clothes and a bunk bed in Ziona's room. When questioned, she said, "There are no gender roles in my home and my daughter can wear anything she wants," which is beautiful and amazing parenting, but as for the bunk bed...that still remains a mystery. The evidence does to this day lean towards there being another child but recently, her birth records went missing. Now there is no telling what could be going on since our amazing police officers are unable to gather evidence correctly. A few years ago, Grandma Zira claimed that Kindal was being bullied and abused by his mother which is why he has scars and why she is denying him. However, with Zira's history of being deranged, prone to lying, and severe cases of schizophrenia, her word is on the back burner. The only word that could break this case is Ziona's, but sadly, she went missing three days after the police started their investigations - which just so happened to be the night of her golden birthday. Her disappearance is unknown for now, but her mother wants to mark this as death.

So, for the few of you that believe this boy exists, keep on believing. Not a day goes by where we don't miss Ziona. She was our only hope in solving our town's biggest mystery. Ever since she went missing on her 22nd birthday, everyone seems to go missing on their golden birthdays. She has been pronounced dead.

A time that once was a widespread celebration in this town has now spread fear in anyone celebrating.

Two Children Found Today

BY: KC Bluesea

***The first child**, a Middle schooler by the name of Obeah Green, was recently pronounced dead after being found face down floating at Sortileges Lake two days after her 13th birthday. Her family, who went on vacation like many parents do when their kids have their golden birthdays, claim that she was perfectly normal when they left. Their house is nowhere near the lake.*

Mrs. Aizlyn, a forensic scientist that is working closely with our investigations unit, says that the drowning was staged. Obeah was dead hours before she was found floating in the lake. With no froth being around her mouth and nostrils, it was found that she could have died from fire. Fire that she surprisingly should have died from in a matter of ten minutes due to high heat exposure.

***The second child** was found that same night hanged in the fishing shack by Sortileges Lake. The family says that their child, Jinx Nabra, went over to Obeah's house that night to celebrate her birthday with her. Sadly, none of them survived, just like the thousands of other townsfolk celebrating their birthdays. All of their death locations were nowhere near their homes and a few deaths, like Obeah, were staged. Police officers have connected some of the deaths together due to friends and family of the birthday children celebrating with them. However, the disappearances, killings, and murders in regards to these birthday deaths are advancing. No one knows how this is happening. Conspiracy theories are waving around the town and are in our Crystal View Supernatural news articles. Over a decade has passed. As of today we have four birthday survivors - names won't be disclosed for legal reasons, but this is a small town so you can figure it out. These people are keeping quiet about their experiences, so please don't bombard them. Be respectful of their traumas.*

Their ages and when their event happened are listed below. This much we can disclose.

Two males, both 15 years old now, had celebrated their Golden birthday a decade after Obeah. One celebrated at age 9 and the other at 15.

The other two, who are friends, celebrated together twice, and are both 13 now. One girl had hers at 6 and the other was 12. Sadly, they both passed away four years later when camping.

Happy Early Death Day {Lowell}

The clock reads nine p.m. as my sister, Lilian, walks into the club. She is wearing her black skimpy dress and five-inch red heels. We both work here doing different jobs, and even though it is required, I don't wear the uniform being a short black dress for women. Instead, I always wear a black t-shirt with cuffed black jeans and sneakers which is the men's typical uniform.

Lilian walks over, sits down, and modestly crosses her legs on a barstool in front of me. She is waiting for her boyfriend. Constantly checking her phone to pass time. They meet here at nine-thirty every other day, so they can hang out in one of the lounge rooms before she starts her shift.

I try to be supportive since he makes her happy, but they shouldn't be together. They constantly get into fights, and she cheats on him afterward. I love my sister, but they should just break up so he can find someone better.

The bar glows with pink and gold lights. Ladies walk around carrying drinks, and men try to flirt with them. I don't drink alcohol since I'm underage but can serve because I'm eighteen.

For the next thirty minutes, guys constantly walk up to Lilian to get her number while they look at me with confused expressions. Most people don't approach me. Either because they've gotten used to me saying no to their questions or they just don't know my gender and are scared to ask.

Boredom fills the room. The clock's hands turn slowly.

Nine-thirty rolls around, and my sister leaves with her boyfriend. Other coworkers start to clock out and head home. I, however, continue to serve drinks for the next thirty minutes, watching the disco ball change between blue and silver lights.

Just as the clock hits ten, I get up and go to the other side of the bar counter. Sitting on a stool. No one is in the bar right now, since our DJ plays the best songs between ten and eleven. If someone worked with me in this department, nights like this wouldn't be so lonely.

I clean the glasses. Trying not to drop them on the rosewood floor as a girl walks up to me.

She is wearing a long-sleeve white crop top that shows a small amount of midriff. Her black skinny jeans and combat boots complement her light brown skin. The disco lights from the dance floor bounce off her shirt.

She stares at me with a pure expression as she sits on the barstool. I walk over to the other side of the counter to put the glasses back in the cabinet. She doesn't say anything to me, perhaps split this into two she just stares. At first, she sizes me up with a straight face. But smiles every time we make eye contact with each other. Blushing, I stand in front of her and dry off a glass.

"Would you like something to drink?" I ask as she looks at me.

I can tell she is underage, but I want to see what she will say. A lot of people, underaged or with false IDs, come in here and try to order a drink. After working here for two years, I realized that there are no rules for our age limit when we work here unless you are a bartender, so many 16+ friends show up just because they can. Our lounge area in the back offers alcohol-free drinks for teenagers. The lounge is a separate building that was made a year ago due to our growing population of teenagers, and it connects to this one through a hallway.

"I'm underage. Though, if you worked as the lounge bartender-" she sizes me up with her eyes, "I would get a drink." She smiles, placing her phone face down on the counter.

"How old are you?" I ask out of curiosity.

"18."

She then releases her hair out of its ponytail and lets her curls fall. Her beauty almost kills me as her curls lay on her shoulders. I clear my throat as a way to get out of my thoughts. She glances at me and takes a step back as if to not make me uncomfortable because I cleared my throat.

"What's wrong?"

She makes eye contact. Her beautiful dark brown eyes hold stars. "Nothing."

I stand there looking for something to do as she looks at the dance floor. She seems nervous, like she is trying to hide from someone. Her hand shakes slightly as she bounces her leg.

"How old are you?" she asks, putting her gaze back on me.

"I'm also 18, but I'll be 19 in a couple of days. Golden birthday things."

"That's cool. Happy early birthday then." She looks at me. "Also, I'm sorry, in my head I assumed you were a woman. Are you?"

I pause.

She's perfect… but why would she say that? I said I was having a golden birthday soon but instead of leaving the scene as quickly as possible, she said happy early birthday. Perhaps that's what the August weather does to you. The leaves are turning brown, and wind is starting to howl so loud that you get used to not fully listening to people's words.

With a confused smile I say, "Yes. I am."

She grins at me while looking back at the dance floor a second time. She is hiding from someone.

"What are you looking for?" I ask, sitting on the stool next to her.

Before she can answer, I see a guy look at us. Causing the girl to dart behind me. Crawling under the stool as he passes. She quickly thanks me as the guy fully passes us, and she sprints out of the door. I look at the guy again, but he doesn't talk to me. He just goes back to the dance floor.

I then get up to clock out of work. That's when the girl's phone catches my eye. She had left it on the counter. I run to the doors to see if she is outside, but she is gone. Placing the phone in my pocket, I switch shifts with an A.M. bartender. Looking at my phone, I wait by the doors for my sister so we can head home.

It is midnight and I must get ready to move into my dorm in 16 hours.

The streetlights are on. The stars are glowing brightly.

There is little traffic, but it still takes us an hour and a half to get back home. When we pull up into the driveway, I park the car next to my mom's and climb out. Lilian wraps her arms around my shoulder as her face gets paler. She is stumbling while we walk up the steps to our porch.

I unlock the door.

The house is quiet, and all the lights are off. I lay Lilian on the couch on her side, and head to the kitchen to get her water. Being nice, I throw the water bottle at her from the kitchen, and she starts to cry. I just laugh as I walk over and pull her hair back with an extra hair tie I had on my wrist. She then throws up all over my shirt and laughs as I push her off me in anger. I almost didn't hear my mom walking downstairs because she was laughing and crying so loud.

"I'll take it from here, sweetheart. Take a shower and go to bed."

She then air hugs me because of the vomit on my shirt.

I head upstairs to my room. Glancing around and gathering my clothes, I head to the bathroom. Cutting off one of the lights so that the room is dim, I lay my clothes on the counter. I then toss my shirt into the dirty clothes basket that we assign to puke stains and pull back the shiny blue shower curtain. I find it relaxing to take a shower in a dimly lit room with the bathroom door locked as soothing music plays in the background.

When I get out of the shower, I take the rest of my dirty clothes to my personal dirty clothes basket and finish packing for college.

It is cold as the ceiling fan blows around; my arms have goosebumps. I take the girl's phone out of my pants pocket and lay it on my bed. She doesn't a passcode on her phone so I take a picture of myself and go back to staring at her lock screen - it's a purple broken heart image on a rainy-day backdrop. A collage just like mine except hers expresses "anxiety" and "it's all in your head."

As I am mesmerized by the details in the broken heart, her screen goes black again. I toss the phone in my jacket pocket.

After a while of staring at the ceiling, my dog jumps on my bed and sits on my legs.

"I'm going to miss you, Luna." She licks my face and farts at the end of my bed. "Eww," I laugh, pushing her over while rubbing her head.

My legs fall asleep due to her laying on them. I then pick up my phone and dial Christopher's number.

"Good night," he says in a deep, tired voice. I smile on my end of the phone. He forgets that most people take that as an "I'm leaving" type greeting.

"I made a friend, I think."

"And…"

"And she's nice. Seems to not know what a golden birthday is, and… I have her lost phone."

"You stole her phone so you could return it and ask her to play your birthday game of death?" he replies, confused. "That is messed up."

"No, she left it at the club after talking to me. Though I will be returning it," I add in a chipper tone. "I'm kind of happy now since we're getting more players and-"

"We need to speak before the game," he sighs, interrupting. "I'm having an issue with playing."

The phone then clicks off.

I look at Luna. We both share a "What was that?" glance because Christopher never hangs up on me.

With my happiness now killed, Luna lays her head on my lap. Blood is now running down her eyes.

Worried, I touch her face but when I glance at my hands, there is no blood.

Rubbing my eyes, I look back at her.

She looks normal.

Don't Go Missing {Xena}

"I CAN'T FIND IT!" I shout as my mom walks down the stairs with my boxes.

"Find what?"

"My phone. When I left the club yesterday I didn't feel it in my pockets, so I just figured I left it at home, but it is not here. I hope it's still at the club because I can't afford to replace it."

"You went to the club yesterday?" My mom asks while placing the box back on the floor.

She gives me a death stare and waits for my response.
"Mom, that's beside the point. I can't move into my dorm without my phone."

I grab my blanket and place it in one of the open boxes. I then pick the box up and carry it to the car as my mom follows me, laughing. She almost falls down the rosewood stairs from cry-laughing so hard at my misfortune.
"It's not funny. I'm serious," I pout as she hands me the box in her hands.

"Serves you well. I told you not to stay out that late. Besides, you need to leave anyway so I can straighten up the house. I invited Captain J over," she grins.

Done packing up the car, I slide my hoodie on over my tank top and climb into the driver's seat.
"I'm going to pretend like you didn't say that last part involving Richard's dad. With that being said, can you please look for my phone!?" I plead,

starting the car up. I want to get to my dorm before my roommate so I can choose my side, but how can I contact my mom if I don't have my phone?

"I'll check. Though are you sure you don't want me to come with you? Kids have been going missing these days-"

"I know…"

"Five teenagers went missing on someone's birthday because they played a game," we say simultaneously. She rolls her eyes at me, knowing that she says that anytime she possibly can.

"Something that only happens in this town, I guess," I add as she gives a worried look. "Mom, I will be fine. Besides, you and Captain J already threatened Richard and me about staying safe and protecting one another."

"I know Richard will keep you safe, but Richard's dad and I can still be worried. You're my only child and I ain't 'bout to have no more kids if you go missing," she laughs.

I laugh while copying the hand gestures she used when making that statement. I then wave her goodbye and pull the car out of the driveway. My first thought is that leaving will be easy, but the more distant my red two-story house gets, the more nervous I become.

The drive is three hours on the main interstate, but it will take me two since I'm going down the backroads. There is no traffic on them and it's almost a straight shot. To keep my energy, I eat road snacks I brought from home and drink the soda I got when I stopped at the gas station earlier.

After a while of easy traffic, the cars start to get congested. The campus is close.

As I look out of the window, I see the college on my right.

It is a huge, red-bricked building with stained glass windows on the roof. Signs are directing the freshmen to the east wing, and there are flags with the school's name on the front. I didn't realize that the Crystal View Academy of Fine Arts was such a beautiful school in person.

I follow the rest of the cars into the parking area, but there are no available spots, so I park across the street from the school. Just as this guy walks towards my car.

Familiar looking, like my stalker ex, but I avoid eye contact and just watch him leave. He heads down the road, turning into one of the gate entrances to the nearby apartment complexes. I slowly climb out of the car a few minutes after he's out of view.

I then open the trunk of my car and grab one of the boxes.

Making my way through the hallways to my dorm unit, I look at the school map and wander around Floor 3 of the east wing until I see my hallway. The sign above me says "moonlight dreams," so I head down that hallway until I come to dorm C3.

It is quiet as I open the door and walk around looking for my room. Our dorm unit is shaped like a hexagon with 6 rooms at the points, and the kitchen and lounge in the middle. My room is listed as C333, but the last three looked like it was close to falling off of the sign. Opening the door slowly, my roommate isn't noticeably here yet, so I choose to sleep in the bed closest to the door. On the right.

I also love this area because there is a painting on the roof that I admire. It's in an odd spot but it's still nice.

Leaving my box on the bed, I leave to get my other boxes. Three trips from the dorm to my car is how long it took. All I wanted to do was jump onto my bed and take a nap when I got in my room.

Holding the last box tightly in one hand, I twist the key with the other, unlocking the door.

As it opens, I jump, scared. The box falls to the ground. The only thing that could be heard was a shattering noise of the contents inside. Carrying it, I rush over to my bed so I can see what was broken.

I then glare at my roommate.

They are wearing a ski mask over their face.

"I'm sorry I scared you! I'm your roommate, Deondra." She takes the ski mask off and tosses it on her bed. Then we shake hands.

"I'm Xena."

I start taking everything out of the box and see that two of my snow globes have broken. I got them from family trips across the United States, but that doesn't matter anymore. Unbothered, I toss them in the trash and sit on my bed.

"I'm sorry." She apologizes, sitting next to me.

Her skin is as beautiful as the midnight sky, and her short red hair is styled in a curly pixie cut. She looks like a plus-size model from the 50s, especially since she is wearing a red poodle skirt with a black waist band and scarf around her neck. Curvy in all places, she has confidence that few people obtain in their life.

"It's fine, I'm not that materialistic anyways. When did you get here?"

"Hours ago." She then pauses and looks me in the eyes. I don't know why, but my heart races a little faster as she smiles. "I was hanging out with my boyfriend and the guys on the other side of the living room. It was quiet when I arrived so I just hung out in their room until I got bored."

"You're embracing the fact that this is a co-ed dorm unit… I like that-" I pause. Even though it's co-ed, you share a room with someone that is the same gender as you. Paired by the pronouns and gender identity you put on the form. "How long have you and your boyfriend been a thing?"

"For about two months. His name is Mark and he stays in C331 on the other side of the lounge area. I… umm… I am about to leave though. I have to be at work in an hour."

"Okay."

She leaves the room door open when she exits.

After five minutes, she comes back and pokes her head in the doorway.

"Also, you can leave the door open if you don't mind people poking their heads in to introduce themselves. There are no rules in the dorms so feel free to do whatever you like. Except bringing in pets. I'm allergic to dogs and cats."

She then gives me two thumbs ups and leaves for good this time.

I stand up on my bed and hang posters of my favorite 80s shows and fairy lights on the wall behind my bed's headboard. Which light up in a pink, purple and blue ombre. Along with that, I add picture frames, my bedsheets, and push my other boxes under the bed.

After being finished, I throw my backup blanket over my mobile locking chest and sit down on my bed to draw. I look at the white ceiling and gray carpet floor for inspiration but there is none. I then head out of my room and into the lounge to get used to the dorm.

It could spark something.

The lounge has three bean bag chairs, rolling gamer chairs, and a futon couch with a tie-dye carpet in front of it. The stained-glass coffee table has a bowl of fruit in the center (which can be used for still life or eating) and a container of pencils. My favorite part was the 64-inch TV and the easel sitting in the corner of the room.

Bored and tired, I walk over to the futon and lay on it while cutting on cartoons. We have a small open kitchen that you can see from the couch, and there with a cute island in the center. This room is so inspiring, and makes our bedrooms look like a plain canvas to work with.

"I see that you are admiring the room," a guy's voice rings from the kitchen.

I turn around and rest my arms on the back of the couch to look at him. His brown hair is slicked back, and he is wearing an elegant black work vest with a white collared shirt. His pants are black and look like they were ironed 10 times before he left his room earlier today. He smiles at me, making me realize I am sizing him up.

"Classy outfit, chiseled jawline…are you a model?" I smile, as he raises an eyebrow at me. Grinning.

"I was for a couple of years. But I dance now."

"That's cool…I am Xena. An 18-year-old African American artist," I say, scrunching my face at his accent. "What about you, Mr. Dancer?"

"My name is Christopher…I am a 19-year-old Canadian." He breaks my eye contact, nervously. "Though, I was raised here in America since the age of eight."

I then get up off the couch and walk over to him. Stand on my tippy toes to stare into his ocean blue eyes.

"You look hot."

I drop down off my tippy toes, looking back at the TV. His face turns red at my comment, and he places his hands on my shoulders. His face turning redder.

"You are a very bold girl. I like that."

My mouth drops. I then quickly cover my face in embarrassment and move my body backward to make space between us.

"No, I meant you look hot, because of your outfit. Even though you are super sexy, I would never say that to your beautiful face…a-and… I just said the last part out loud, didn't I?"

"Yes, you did, but I can pretend that you didn't. Besides, I am only joking, I like your honesty."

I pause.

"I-, uh…was talking to this woman. You probably won't know her. But afterward, I lost my phone. Feel like she has it, but anyway, can I use your phone to make a call?" I ask aloud.

He raises his eyebrows while moving his gaze off of me, digging his hand in his pocket. Then pulls his phone out. Hands it to me after unlocking it. He takes what feels like 15 seconds to draw the pattern that unlocks his phone.

"Sure."

"Thank you!"

Christopher then starts to fix a cup of water as we both awkwardly stare back and forth at each other. After a couple of minutes of talking to my mom, the call ends. Surprised she even answered. I then hand him his phone back. While Richard comes out of their room. Christopher smiles and slides it back into his pocket.

They both leave the dorm. My heart almost melts as Christopher waves me goodbye. Though I can't help but blow a kiss at Richard. He closes his fist like he caught my kiss while he blows one back.

After the door closes, I run back into my room and start drawing. Inspiration hit me hard.

Know Your Surroundings {Lowell}

As I wake up, I look around my room. I'm impressed with how much I moved in yesterday. My closet is filled with clothes.

Personal bed sheets dress my bed. The theme being blue, I have blue lights hanging from the wall, slippers at the end of my bed, and a blue fuzzy rug on the floor.

I look across the room and notice that my roommate is gone, so I put on my workout clothes. I think I'm going to explore the campus today. Get my mind off of things, since classes don't start until the week after next, in 10 days.

It is quiet as I pull on my sneakers.

Walking through the living room and kitchen area known as "the lounge," I head out of the dorm and down C hall.

The Crystal View Academy of Fine arts is a small school, so mostly everyone from my old high school art/performance art classes is here.

Pulling out a map of the school from my pocket, I try to find the recording studio on it. According to the map, the recording studio is on the west wing, so I would have to take the elevator or stairs down the second floor and head past the library. I then head to the elevator and click the 2nd-floor button. When I get off the elevator I walk across the whole floor until I see a sign that says "West Wing."

A few people pass me down the hallway, but I'm the only one walking alone. Everyone I waved at in the hallway just stared at me with cold eyes. As if you are in a dream and you tell one of the people you see "I know this is a dream" and they glare at you before continuing on with their day.

Creepy.

Yet this has been happening for a few days.

It may be random but part of me found a liking to that girl from the club. If only I could see her more, then maybe I could see if she's okay.

Something's off about her.

Continuing down the hallway on the right side, a sign reading "Library" passes by me. I go farther down the hallway until I come across the room I'm looking for. Then I peek my head in.

The only person that is in there is an African American male, so my feet find themselves guiding me in and my hands close the door behind me.

The room has dotted vinyl flooring and ceiling LED lights across the corners of the room that glow red. A black DJ mixer is on the side of the room farther from the recording studio door, and it looks amazing.

I am about to sit down and spin tracks, but the man's voice distracts me. He has a black business casual top on, black jeans, a brown coat, and a long red scarf laying on his shoulders to tie it all together. Making him look like a rich poet businessman. When he moves his scarf, I see a mark on the top of his chest, but I don't care about it. Leaning against the glass, I listen to his poetic words until he looks at me. He places the headphones over the mic and opens the door.

"I'm sorry, you can use the room if you want to. I've been here for a while already," he mentions in a soothing voice. It is like I could listen to him talk for days.

"You're okay, I was just going to tweak my playlist for later." I shrug. "Your words are very beautiful though. You sounded like you felt them."

"Well, they are personal to me. I was practicing for open mic night next Friday. Are you trying to come…?" He pauses, raising his eyebrow.

"Lowell," I reply, introducing myself. He holds his hand out and I shake it. "It may not look like it, but I am a woman."

He then shakes his hands making the "so-so" gesture, meaning that I pull off both.

"Nice to meet you, Lowell. My name is Richard. And I am a man," he says, handing me a flyer. "You should come though."

He then opens the door and leaves the studio.

Weird energy follows behind him. Some of that energy lingering around me.

Maybe I should have told him to stay longer, but my brain won't tell me why he needs to be here.

I look at the flyer to figure out how far away the date is. It says it's in 13 days. *He must like to be prepared,* I think to myself while folding the flyer and sliding it in my pocket. Or maybe he just doesn't procrastinate like I do. I then sit down in the chair and start working on my remixes. The lights turn various colors as I beat match the songs and speed up the tempo.

Hours pass.

Just as I finish, I turn it off and leave the room.

Walking down the hallway, I head back to my dorm unit. I open the door and step onto the colorful carpet flooring.

It's confusing but my hunches are telling me to remember that the front door is in between rooms C331 and C332 in this hexagon-looking dorm unit. My room, C334, is one out of two rooms farthest from the door.

As I walk through the lounge and the kitchen, my eyes gaze upon a familiar face walking into their room. I recognize the back of her. It is the girl who left her phone yesterday at the club.

Too scared to walk over to her, I quickly dart into my room and trip over the rug in front of the door. I decided to write a note for her and drop it off with the phone at her room door, which happens to be right next to mine. I then look at my phone.

Work starts in three hours, so I knock on her door and leave the note before she opens it.

I dart back into my room only to see my roommate, Zoe, sitting on her bed reading a book. Her legs are crossed, and she looks up at me through her glasses. My eyes trail down to the front of her pants. I swallow hard.

"Are you okay?" I ask. She looks at me with a confused look. She places her book down and stands up.

"I'm good."

My face makes a weird expression in disbelief. I then wave my finger at her pants, hoping she can see the blood too.

She then looks down and sees a huge red stain on her white jeans. Embarrassed, she tries to figure out what to do.

"Oh geez. Oh geez. This is real."

She paces back and forth talking to herself out loud. "I can't go to the bathroom because the other people in our dorm unit will see me. Though if I walked out with a blanket over myself then no one will know…wait, I can't do that because that's weird. Maybe I should just make a run for it."

She starts freaking out even more, so I walk over and place my hands on her shoulder to stop her.

"The blanket idea wasn't that bad. Besides, no one was out there when I first came in so you should be good. You act like this is your first cycle," I laugh, as she wraps a small blanket over her waist.

"I'm flustered is all," she says, covering up her yellow bracelet.

“Though I was a late bloomer, so I haven't been worrying about this for that long."

"Oh okay. Well, I'm about to leave for work. Have fun with your little…situation," I sarcastically reply. Thinking to myself that she'd be terrible if I asked her to play my birthday game.

Zoe just looks at me with a surprised facial expression as her blond hair hangs over her face. She doesn't say anything as I pull my black shirt on over my sports bra. She just stares at me and smiles before walking out of the door to go to the bathroom. Shrugging, I finish changing and leave for work.

Once I get off the campus lawn, I drive an hour to work and park in the my employee's parking spot. Then head into the building and clock into work.

The club is quiet. The lights are not on yet. Most people don't come here and party until nine, so the first hour is me waiting and talking to the DJ and my best friend Christopher. I met them when we first started working here a year ago, and we just clicked. DJ just so happens to be our DJ and Christopher is the runner who serves drinks in the dancing area.

I skip over to the DJ stand on stage to see if the DJ is there. Since he hasn't arrived and the stand is unoccupied, I decide to spin my tracks. Only two songs anyway.

"So, are you going to DJ with me tonight? We shouldn't let your talent go to waste," he yells, walking up to the stand to join me. Nearly scaring me half to death.

Christopher of course follows behind him but stops and stands in the middle of the dance floor.

"Give me a beat," Christopher laughs, getting ready to dance on the empty floor.

I roll my eyes and play the mix I was working on earlier as Christopher dances along. DJ and I laugh at Christopher taking his best attempt at hip-hop, even though we know he is better at ballet.

"Lowell, you should DJ with me tonight. The people will love you," he yells again while putting the headphones over his neck.

"You know if I do that I will get fired. Besides, I don't mind bartending, and I can't promise that I will still be living by the time he thinks about offering me a DJ position."

"I don't want you to lose your job, but you should let people hear your talent. You are amazing."

He then pokes my nose as I walk off the stage.

Wiping my nose softly, smiling.

I can see the people starting to pour in, so I sprint over to the bar. Jumping across the counter. My manager glares at me and just rolls his eyes. He hates that I do that.

"I need you to train one of our new employees."

"Are they going to be a bartender?"

"That's none of your concern. If you die in a few days then I'll need another hand…so train her well."

I roll my eyes in anger as he waves for her to come over. He then walks off towards the lounge as the girl looks at me, nervously twiddling her fingers. Sometimes I just want to punch him in the throat. So hard that he tastes his own blood. But if I did that then we all would be without a job.

Though coincidentally, it is the girl from yesterday. We live in a town-sized city so I'm not too surprised to see her working in the only club in town and going to the same fine arts school around here. But it does confuse me that of all the places, she chose to work in this building. I hate to assume, but I doubt she's here for the same reason as me. It just makes this more fun I guess.

"Hey, I'm glad to see you again for the second time today. I'm Lowell."

We share a passionate glance.

"Umm… I'm Xena."

"Xena… that's a pretty name."

"Almost as pretty as you, but thank you! Shall we get started?"

"We shall. But I have one question first," I blush.

"What's up?"

"I returned your phone, and you show up as my new coworker. Come on?" I raise an eyebrow.

"Oh, yeah, it was love at first sight and I just had to get this job so I could see you more," she teases dramatically. I roll my eyes.

Hopefully it's too dark for her to see my rosy red cheeks.

"I'm joking. My friend Richard helped me get this job weeks ago. I was already supposed to start today because the boss said that he would need to fill the position fast. So fast that he didn't ask me for anything, just told me to show up."

She then smiles while taking her jacket off. Tying it around her waist.

It's understandable that he's anticipating me dying, but can he not say it to my face? It's scary.

I then roll my sleeves back.

Before the crowd comes into the bar, I explain the basic information on working the machines, cleaning glasses, and where to put everything. After the 10-minute lesson, everyone comes in, so she must start working.

"Hey, you're fine. I'm right here if you come into trouble," I say, patting her shaking hand.

She just looks away, nodding her head, while rubbing her other hand over mine for a quick second. We then let go.

The club is louder today than it was yesterday. Though that's probably because we offer free entry to everyone before 11. Saturday's themes are blue, so the disco light is shining blue for most of the night and green at one point.

For the next few minutes, Xena spills three drinks on me and breaks 7 glasses, but she is learning fast overall. As long as she doesn't get any of the customers, we are good. It's not like the manager needs to know anyway.

We continue working for a while when this man shows up. Xena is taking orders right now and mopping up her mess so we won't fall, while I am in the back getting us more glasses. I carry three glasses to the counter as the guy stands up and yells at her. I don't know what she did, but he looks like he's about to fight her. Something that I don't tolerate at all.

"WATCH WHAT YOU'RE DOING YOU DUMB-"

"Woah, calm down," I interrupt quickly. In a joking tone. Placing the glasses on the counter.

"No! She needs to come over here and clean it off," He bellows reaching over the counter grabbing Xena's arm. This behavior usually only happens to the existing staff members like myself. Never to the newbies and never over spilled drinks.

"I'm sorry," Xena apologizes, snatching her wrist away hard to free herself.

She accidentally crashes into me, causing us to fall against the wall next to the machines. Everyone starts staring at us as the man laughs, grabbing his cup. Knocking over other glasses and drinks, he pours the remaining liquid of his and someone else's glass before walking away. His entourage leaves with him.

The bar is completely empty now.

Sighing deeply, I lean the back of my head against the wall. Xena helps me up.

It feels weird having alcohol running down my hair, but I try to keep it together. Unlike Xena, who looks like she's on the verge of breaking down into tears.

"I'm sorry. I didn't mean to knock into you or spill the drink on the guy."

"It's fine. The guy was drunk anyway, so don't let it bother you. If it weren't for this job, I would have started a fight," I reassure.

Xena still looks upset.

"I guess. But I shouldn't even have this job. I can't seem to do anything right. You know, dropping 7 glasses and spilling three drinks like a dumba-"

"Actually, this would make four. Four drinks," I interrupt.

"Even worse," she sighs, walking away to the back room.

For the rest of the night, Xena doesn't talk to me, and she has a sad facial expression. When our shift ends, she clocks out first and leaves immediately afterward.

I know she is a clumsy person and shouldn't have even made it past training if our boss wasn't so desperate, but I hate seeing my co-workers sad. Especially since I heard her crying in the women's bathroom when I walked by earlier.

Something's telling me that it's not just about the spilled drink.

I just know that if I see that guy again, it won't be pret

Treasure Hunting {Lowell}

It is the night before my birthday and my hand shakes slightly while my heart races just thinking about it.

I sit on Christopher's bed waiting for him.

Richard, the poet I met in the studio, sits on his bed writing in his journal. We sit in awkward silence. I just found out that he was Christopher's roommate.

Staring off into space, my brain conjures up the imagery of fire on the walls. Orange and yellow light fills the room. Blocking the door. Instead of being scared, I stare at it. Captivated by the way the flames dance next to each other. Coming closer to my feet.

"Sorry for the wait. I had to make a call," Christopher announces, slamming the door closed behind him.

The sound knocks me back into reality. The fire goes away in a blink. Christopher avoids my eye. Looking at Richard.

He then comes and sits down next to me as I lean against the wall.

"Christopher, I need you!"

He looks down at my lap, not responding. Richard then looks up from his journal for a split second. Trying not to pry into our conversation.

"I am still going to be there for you. I only said there was an issue because I was battling my memories of celebrating my own game."

I frown.

"Oh."

"It is fine though. What is your favorite game supposed to be anyway?"

"Well, the game is treasure hunting. I've loved it since I was a kid..."

I start to look at the floor. My words finding their way into changing the subject.

"Did you ever start seeing things before your golden birthday? Like blood. Or fire?"

"Yes, I did. More often as the day of my birthday crept close," he whispers back, grabbing a pen and paper out of his backpack.

Christopher then proceeds to write down eight names, including ours.

Leaving a little bit of space for details.

Richard glances up at me again. His eyes stare deep into my soul this time, causing me to break eye contact. Footsteps cross under the slit in the door. Our other roommates talk outside in the main room.

In silence, Christopher and I sit.

Writing out the plan to get everyone here and what we would need to get for tomorrow.

A loud knock on the door interrupts our writing.

"Come on in," Christopher yells.

I then frowned at him.

"What? We can take guests now," he whispers to me as Xena walks into the room.

She is wearing an oversized lightning bolt t-shirt and knee-length mushroom socks.

"Hey, Christopher. Lowell…Richard." She acknowledges the group, yawning. Slightly smiling after saying Richard's name. We all then yawn in response to watching her yawn.

"Nice socks," I compliment.

She wiggles her toes while replying, "Thank you. See, they match the mushrooms on your shirt, I didn't know that."

I then look at my shirt, smiling.

They do.

"Is there something wrong?" Richard asks, moving to the edge of his bed. Placing his feet on the carpet.

"Can I borrow a jacket? Preferably one that you wore recently."

He then lets out a quick breath and smiles widely. Pointing at the tall dresser on his side of the room. He has a jacket lying on the top.

"I thought it was an emergency."

"It is," she laughs, "I can't sleep."

He then raises an eyebrow.

"It looks nice on you. Keep it if you'd like."

"Planned on it, boo."

She then waves us bye. Closing the door softly.

Christopher stands up and stretches. Handing me the paper he was writing. Richard then looks over at me again.

"Do you have something to say?" I snap, slightly annoyed at the constant staring.

"No. But if the fire you see turns red, run. Leave the room as quickly as possible, even if it's not burning anything," he replies, standing up.

"What do you know?"

"I know that if you decide to stay in the room, the smoke produced will silently kill you from the inside out."

I raise an eyebrow, slightly believing him. His face is cold and serious.

"How do you know that? Have you had your golden birthday yet?" I question.

He glances over his shoulder with lifeless eyes.

"Yes…and I learned from experience."

He then closes the door. Leaving Christopher and me in the room alone.

What a weird roommate. Christopher smiles awkwardly from the exchange Richard and I just had and takes the paper back.

I remain quiet.

He starts to explain to me that Richard had celebrated his golden birthday years ago and is one of the few survivors in this town. He has been alone in life ever since except for Xena being his friend. I'm guessing that he and Richard related to "being alone in life," which is why he knows so much about him now.

Richard is mysterious, but I can't believe that he learned from experience. If he claims the red fire kills, then how could he learn that if he's still here? He's not dead. However, as a person who knows nothing about what goes on during the night of golden birthdays, I want Richard there. His demeanor is cold and distant, but he knows something.

That could be important.

Besides, glancing at Christopher's paper, he put everyone in this dorm as a possibility. Xena included. So maybe we can get Richard to join if she says yes.

"Do you think Richard and Xena are dating?"

I shrug.

"I don't know. I might die tomorrow; I'm not worried about other people's relationship statuses right now."

"Of course. It just seems weird that Xena has been so jumpy, is all. I am just concerned about her. At work, she seems to get clingy with me when people flood the dance floor."

"Maybe she likes you," I joke, yawning.

Knowing that he hates it when I tell him that there are people that do form crushes on him. In his words, he finds it "repugnant."

Christopher shrugs. His eyes then lock onto Richard's bed.

"I think something is amiss in your assumptions, but it won't hurt to point it out to her. Though, it may have to do with something else, Lowell."

My brain drifts off into what happened during her training day. With the guy at the counter. It was the same guy she seemed to be running from the first day I met her.

With Christopher's theory, I "might need to have a little chat with that man from the club."

He could be right about it having to do with anything else. And since I'm going to die tomorrow, I might as well make a little mischief. Wouldn't hurt.

Broken Bones {Xena}

Sunshine creeps through the window, blinding my eyes as I roll over on my back.

It's about 10 A.M.

Looking over at Deondra's bed, she is gone. I then check my phone and I see a personal message from Lowell. Almost forgot that Christopher created a dorm unit group chat, so I have her number on my phone. We just don't talk outside of the group chat. And ever since she returned my phone, I haven't been on it much.

I sit up and stretch, cutting off my fairy lights. Stepping onto the soft grey carpet, sliding my feet into my slippers. Lowell and I haven't had a decent, long conversation since my training day 5 days ago. We see each other at work every day but our manager moved me, so now I'm a runner with Christopher.

I get embarrassed and nervous when around her. Sometimes because her smile makes me nervous. And other times because she actually cares about my well-being for some odd reason. Though I'm mostly distant since that guy won't leave me alone and he started messing with Lowell.

It is easier to be distant than to risk her safety.

Tired, I open the bedroom door and walk to the lounge.

BING!

A notification from Richard pops up on my phone. Curious, I click the video link he sent me. It plays.

It's Lowell, from what I can see, fighting someone. The other person is screaming. It sucks that I can't see it completely. Whoever filmed this fight didn't know that the camera should be pointed at the fight. Not everywhere else. Like there is no reason for them to be shaking so much, it's literally right in front of them.

Annoyed by the lack of information and the cameraman, I head into the kitchen to find Lowell. Then I see her. All of her for once.

She is cooking and cutting fruits on the granite countertop. Her back is turned to me, and her short brown hair is pulled back into a ponytail. A smile spreads across my face. She is wearing a white fitted tank top, blue sweatpants, and fuzzy slippers.

"So how bad did you beat that guy up? The video doesn't show much," I ask Lowell, while I sit down in one of the four chairs at the island.

She frowns and ignores my question. Not looking at me.

"Fine. Different question - how did the fight start?"

She sighs and then sets her cup on the counter. It makes a loud noise.

"I followed the guy outside one day and told him that if he ever talked to you or tried to grab your wrist again, I'd beat him up. He thought I was messing with him, so he pushed me onto his car, it escalated, and I broke his arm. Self-defense is my alibi," she discloses, turning around.

Facing my way.

I nod, looking at her with soft eyes as she leans over the island counter. Her ivy-green eyes pierce into my soul. Making me feel warm inside. I then poke her nose and laugh as she sticks out her tongue, scrunching her nose.

Trying my hardest to bottle up my happiness, I hold my hands behind my back, rocking forward.

"So, uh…why?" I say, glancing at the floor.

Her face then drops slowly. Guilty.

She probably thinks that I'm disappointed in her fighting people. Honestly, her aggression doesn't bother me completely. It's hard to explain but as long as she doesn't hit me in anger, I'm fine. She's just protective. As for aggressive *guys*…nope. Hell no. I'll pass regardless and will always be triggered. I don't care.

"I don't care that you fought him. I think that was very brave of you, yet…stupid," I add.

She smiles.

"I don't know..." she pauses, almost at a loss for words, but she clears her throat. "I just don't like it when my friends are sad and distant from me. Besides, I love working with you as a bartender…if he stays around then you'll never come back."

She shrugs after saying that.

I let out a faint smile.

Feeling strong love in my heart for her, but not knowing why.

Gathering my broken thoughts, I find myself stuck.

"Are you bothered by what I said?" I ask.

She bites her lips, curling them in her mouth. Making a weird face.

"No." she smiles with no teeth, messing up my hair. "It's nothing."

"Yeah right, it's nothing."

I then stare at her. Lowell's face grows tough, and her eyes narrow as if she is upset.

"When I said it was stupid, I wasn't talking about your intellect. I was talking about how you could have seriously gotten hurt by him. Also, you could have gotten arrested."

She chuckles in amusement.

"Thank you for your concern but I don't need it. I've always been good on my own," Lowell replies, coldly. "Though…if he does something to you, or anyone for that matter, then tell me. I can deal with it."

Glancing away, she then looks back at the fruit. Holding her bowl out for me to take one.

I ponder over the fact that she claims she's "always been good on her own." In my experience, it's a sign of neglect in one's childhood. She may not have ever had someone protect her, so she feels the need to be the protector even if scared.

"N-No, thank you, I'm good."

I then twiddle my fingers.

She shrugs and places a cube of pineapple in her mouth.

A small wave of happiness fills me as I think about the fact that she broke his arm. My hand unknowingly flaps in excitement. Lowell raises an eyebrow, confused.

I try to suppress my happiness but it's overwhelming.

"Are you..."

"Can I hug you?" I ask, interrupting her.

Her eyes grow wide, and her cheeks slightly turn red.

"Uh, sure."

Smiling, I hug her for a few seconds.

The feeling of her heartbeat relaxes me. Her arms wrap around my back slowly. But before she fully embraces me, I break the hug.

I then thank her before skipping off to my room.

Closing the door behind me, I start to freak out with excitement. I forgot how nervous I get when I talk to her. "Good job, me." I do a little happy dance before running toward my closet.

Relaxing hours pass as I draw. We don't have work tonight, but I have an outfit out for later tonight.

Just as my sketchbook finds its way inside my drawer, Christopher calls me.

"Good afternoon," he says when I answer the phone.

"Hey, what's up?"

Christopher and I do talk and text each other all the time outside of the group chat. Usually with clothing advice or asking each other if we want to go on shopping trips.

"Would you like to go to the store with me? I have to get a few things."

"Sure."

"Okay, then meet me in the lobby in ten minutes."

"Give me twenty."

"Okay."

We both then go quiet. I don't hang up because I'm putting my drawing materials away. I walk away from the phone but he's on speaker because Deondra isn't in the room.

Christopher then clears his throat. I thought he would have hung up by now.

"Are you taking my kindness as something more than kindness?"

My eyebrows push inward, confused.

"If you're asking if I have feelings for you, then no. I don't. Why?"

"Because lately, we have always been around each other. Usually, when women say yes to me all the time and enjoy the feminine part of me, which I heavily embrace, it is because they want something. I know the bar for men is low. Technically speaking, you say it's 'on the floor,' but I do not want you to mistake my kindness as me liking you."

"Yes. The bar is on the floor," I laugh. "Many girls would definitely like you because you are respectful and understanding, I get that, but I don't have feelings for you either. I just see that part of you as welcoming. Truly we are friends and if there were to be more going on, I feel like us two, of all people, would know that."

"Yes."

"But don't worry Christopher, I'm not interested. And I know that you aren't either. I just like being around you, okay?"

"Me too. I like being around you. You give off amazing energy."

"Thank you! As do you."

We then say our goodbyes.

He is an overthinker, I know, but adorable nonetheless.

I hang up the phone and start changing into my clothes. Pulling my hair back in a ponytail and grabbing my tiny backpack, I walk out of my room. Then sit on the couch and wait for Christopher to show up.

Looking up at the ceiling, I notice that some of the spots are painted black. Someone's hands then run over my eyes, and I jump slightly.

It goes dark.

"Guess who," a female voice says.

"Telling by the feminine voice and soft hands, it must be Lowell."

"Stop doing that," she whines.

Lowell sits down next to me. She puts her head on my shoulder, with a sad expression on her face.

"What's wrong? Is this about earlier because I'm not sorry for being concerned about your well-being?"

She tries to hold back a smile. "No, that's not it…I just want this day to be over," she sighs, whispering.

"Why?" I question.

Whispering back.

"Nothing…you should just be worried about right now. I wouldn't leave campus if I were you. Today is a dangerous day to be alive. You could..."

Christopher walks into the lounge.

"Never mind," she says, smiling at him and leaving.

He gives her a confused look but lets it slide. More confused, I get up and leave the dorm with Christopher. I have a feeling that tonight is going to be a long night.

We head down to the campus lawn as I zip my jacket up. A couple of other students are hanging out on the huge lawn. The wind is blowing hard as we head to Christopher's car. Traffic is surprisingly low on the main road. However, Lowell's warning of "not leaving campus" sticks in the back of my brain. We leave campus.

All the traffic lights heading to the store are green and it looks like no one is out today. Christopher parks in the empty store parking lot, and I grab his arm before he opens the door. My hands shake slightly and he asks me what is wrong.

"Does Lowell not like her birthdays?"

"It is her golden birthday."

"That's great, but why is she so bothered by it?"

"You will find out later. Just don't get too scared about the events that happen between now and six o'clock."

"Stop beating around the bush. Why would I be scared?" my voice trembles.

He glances into my eyes, quickly looking away.

"Stay in the car."

I can tell that he can sense my paranoid behavior - so he climbs out of the car and locks the doors with me inside. I sit there, watching him walk into the store instead of debating this further. He knows more than he is letting me know, which is something I hate.

They all do.

He is in the store for hours.

My eyes stare at the cars passing through the empty parking lot. For a few minutes someone was practicing parking. Other than that, it is quiet and cold, and the sunny sky is clear of clouds.

A dark spot, noticeable in the distance, creeps close to me.

Clouds roll over the sun. Everything grows grey as I slide into my seat. Ducking as to not be seen. A huge shadow sweeps over the car, making it dark for a while. Then the shadow goes straight over the store and just sits there.

It feels rather weird since clouds are now covering the sun, and it is just sitting over the store. The shadow did what it was doing in less than five minutes.

I stare at it for about ten minutes. Watching it blink light colors of red, blue, and green. Those lights are dots near the center and not the actual color of the shadow.

Shooting Christopher a text to see what was taking him so long, he doesn't answer.

The store lights are now shining blue, but no one seems to even be in the store. I slowly climb over the center console, get out of the car, and walk towards the store. Right before my feet touch the sidewalk in front of the doors, Christopher comes through. I jump out of my skin. He grabs my hand and we walk fast.

I look up and stare at the glowing shadow as we walk back to the car. Both Christopher and I don't talk to each other the whole way home.

All the traffic lights are green. The shadow follows far behind us.

Just as we pass through an intersection, two random cars run, high speed, into each other. Almost like they wanted to.

Christopher slams on the brakes. We both look at the cars behind us upon opening our eyes. They have caught on fire but through the window, we can see that no one is inside. That's when this wave of creepy aura spreads over our car. We see a figure just standing in the middle of the fire.

He looks at me, then back at the figure. It walks off.

Christopher then slams on the gas, speeding back to campus.

He parks the car, grabs the groceries, and we sprint back to our dorm. We close the dorm door behind us, and everyone looks at us as we try to catch our breath.

"Where is Lowell?" Christopher asks, placing the groceries on the counter.

"I don't know," a tall, green-eyed boy replies from the couch.

"Emil, where is she?" Christopher asks once more, trying to stay peaceful.

"She is safe in her room," Zoe answers, walking out of their room.

Christopher then runs into her room and closes the door behind him. After that, it goes quiet.

I glance at Deondra and her boyfriend making out on one of the beanbag chairs. That must be Mark. *And boy does she have good taste,* I think, looking away. He is an Asian male. Judging by his clothes, it's rather obvious that he loves anime like she does.

Tired, I sit next to Richard and ask him if he is still doing the open mic performance tonight. He says no in an upset yet nonchalant tone. I wonder why.

"Okay, so…why is everyone in the lounge right now?" I ask Richard.

Everyone looks at me like I'm crazy. Short silence fills the room.

They then burst out with questions, asking me if I am joking or if I truly didn't know what was about to happen. Zoe remains quiet just like I am at the sudden questioning. All I know is that it's Lowell's birthday and she wants to play a game, but in the way my eyes see it, I don't think that's going to be happening anymore.

"Why are we here?" Deondra asks.

"I'm not joining a cult if that's what it is," Mark adds, jokingly.

"Mm, I could kill for some college excitement. If you know what I mean," Zoe winks, doing a headcount of how many of us are in the room.

Eww, please tell me that's not what this is. Deondra, Mark, and Emil all stare at Zoe with squinted eyes, trying to think of what she may be thinking of. Richard raises an eyebrow in disgust. And I shake my head no. Knowing exactly what she's thinking about.

"Calm down, everyone. And no, Zoe, this is not that kind of group gathering," Richard announces in a soothing voice.

"Well, then what is it?"

"We are here to support Lowell on her…golden birthday, Zoe," Richard hesitates to say.

Everyone then goes quiet.

Their faces grow white as if they saw a ghost or were told their favorite person in the world died.

I'm the only one confused about what a golden birthday is.

What's wrong?

I Made A Mistake {Lowell}

Christopher quickly opens my door and softly closes it behind him. Somehow, he has always been able to keep his composure in situations like these.

"You didn't tell them, did you?"

"I couldn't find the right moment. It's not easy to tell people you just met that they could die on my birthday," I sigh, sitting on my bed.

"They deserve to know the truth and make the choice of whether or not they will play. Everyone needs to make a decision. And we have to start!"

"Fine. I'll tell them right now. Xena's the only person who doesn't know my birthday is…today."

Christopher looks at me with disappointment.

Sighing, he says, "If you weren't fighting death right now, I would continue this pointless argument."

I roll my eyes.

“Okay, I made a mistake and didn't tell you sooner. I just don’t want to get any of you hurt, can we just-”

“Lowell, I said this bickering is pointless. The creature is already here, and we are starting whether you want to or not.”

Christopher then walks out of the room.

I ball my fist, punching the air, before following behind him.

Sitting on the couch across from Xena, Deondra and Mark are still making out for the millionth time today. Emil, Zoe, Richard, Xena, and Christopher all stare at me while I sigh. Nudging Richard so he can explain. Xena's body is positioned closer to him as her knees and feet are pointed at him. Her hands resting in her lap as Christopher takes a few glances at her.

"Our town is more cursed than you would think. If you were born here or moved here then your golden birthday is not the most pleasant day.

Golden birthdays are the day your birth date and age are the same. For example, Lowell is turning 19 and it's August 19th. On your golden birthday, you have to play a game."

"Yes, a 12-hour, or more, game of life or death," I add.

"Are you serious?" Xena interrupts, rolling her eyes.

"Yes. The birthday kid, which would be me in this case, has to play their favorite game. The only catch is you have to have at least four people agree to play with you if it's multiplayer. Or the birthday child automatically dies. It starts close to the time I was born and it would end 12 hours after. Unless you finish early. So, if you start at night then it would end the next morning and vice versa. If any of you agree to play, then you need to know that my favorite game is treasure hunting."

I then look at Xena with a straight face. She nervously laughs covering her mouth.

"Has..."

She clears her throat to hold back her laughter. Smiling.

"…has everyone had their golden birthday already?"

"Just Emil, Christopher, and Richard. Everyone else moved here after their golden birthdays so they didn't have to worry about it."

"Though ninety percent of people who celebrate their golden birthdays die while playing their game. If you don't want to play, then leave this room now before you get locked in," Richard adds aimlessly.

I punch Richard. He rolls his eyes at me.

"That's reassuring," Xena sarcastically replies, raising an eyebrow.

"Okay, well, I'm in," Zoe chimes in a bubbly way.

I think to myself, "Oh, she must want to die," while putting up two thumbs as a response.

"Same here," Mark lies, getting up slowly.

Trying to wave Deondra to follow him out the door. He's trying to leave but Deondra stays sitting.

"Also, Deondra and Mark are in too," Emil volunteers them.

Their jaws then drop while pulling away from each other.

Xena giggles at their reaction as Christopher glances over at her again. A small smile spreads along my face from Xena's soft giggling.

"I don't want to-"

"Shhh," Deondra interrupts Mark. "That's fine. We would love to help you. This isn't my first rodeo."

We look at her, confused.

"I've celebrated these birthdays with my old friends," she adds.

"Oh," we all sigh simultaneously.

Christopher adds, "Of course, you have me," while winking at me.

"Thank you!"

Everyone then looks back and forth between me and Xena, waiting for her to answer. I'm assuming that the only reason everyone agreed is because we all know how hard it is to find people to celebrate with, so I feel better about asking.

"You don't have to play if you don't want to. I already have more than enough-"

"I'm in," she interrupts, shrugging her shoulders.

"Really?" I exclaim, surprised.

"Yes. Don't be so surprised. Somebody has to protect you."

She shrugs again and gets up as Richard smiles. I look her in the eyes, highly doubtful that she can protect me. But she is in so it doesn't matter.

"Then you got me too. No odd numbers," Richard shrugs.

Xena then smiles and messes up his hair with her hands.

I look away. Thinking to myself, *Yes!,* Christopher shares a "thank goodness" glance at me.

We all then slowly start standing up, ready for what is about to happen.

We scatter around for a few minutes, calming our nerves.

Mark tried to leave the room three times, but Deondra and Emil kept dragging him back in.

Richard ran around the house filling up his backpack; I slid my sneakers on. I add some of the groceries from Christopher's shopping trip to the bag, none involving food - just survival things like batteries, bandages, and things of that sort. Many things he couldn't find in the store.

During all of the commotion, Richard doesn't lay an eye on me. Yet every time I walk close to him, he moves over, making space between us.

Xena is the only person who he lets in his bubble. He gravitates towards her naturally, like a bodyguard almost.

After what feels like thirty minutes of craziness, the lights cut off. Emil slowly creeps over to the switch and tries to turn them back on.

No use.

"I guess we are starting now," he sadly announces.

We all then huddle back-to-back in the middle of the room.

Dark and quiet. All eight of us tremble.

The coffee table moves close to me. The room lights turn blue. The scary spirit thing is here.

My body goes stiff.

With a stack of cards on the table, I slowly reach for the top card and read it aloud. My voice on the edge of breaking.

It reads:

"The objective of treasure hunting is to follow the riddles and make it to the end. You will split up into groups of four that will slowly decrease as the game progresses. You must complete the game by sunrise, or you lose. Good luck!"

"I know the thing did not just tell us good luck. Like that is so creepy," Zoe rebukes in a snobby rich girl tone.

My eyes roll as I pick up the next card.

Everyone hovers around me.

"This card says that we need to get in a group of four, but we don't get to choose. I don't understand what that means," I say, putting it back on the table.

Once I let the card go, the lights cut off.

Zoe screams and someone grabs my wrist. Though I am unaware of who grabbed me, my focus is on the tiny blue light moving around the eight of us. Abruptly stopping right in front of Emil.

As quickly as it comes, the light grows bigger and bigger before exploding. Throwing all eight of us into the wall.

After a few seconds of silence, soaking in the pain, the lights go back to normal. Cutting back on. My spine is hurting, but I was lucky enough to hit the wall with nothing on it. Probably just a light bruise on my back. It all happened so quickly that none of us had the time to scream.

While helping Christopher and Zoe up, I see Deondra, Mark, Richard, and Xena on the opposite side of the room. These must be our groups.

"AHHHH!!!" Zoe screams, high-pitched, running over to Emil.

Christopher and Deondra cover their ears as if they can hear ringing. Blood on Deondra's forehead from impact, and blood coming out of Mark's ear.

That screaming echoes through the room, catching all our attention.

Emil is lying on the floor gasping for air. Blood pouring out of his body like a waterfall. Puddling around him. The top of the easel stand is completely through his stomach.

Deondra throws up at the sight of his blood and runs to the bathroom. Freaking out.

Xena is holding Zoe back so she won't touch him, as Zoe is ugly crying over his now lifeless body.

"I guess we did need an odd number," Mark laughs.

We all then sharply glare at him. Zoe is still crying.

He jumps. Scared.

"Loosen up guys. Can't you take a joke?" he replies, walking to the bathroom to comfort his girlfriend.

He walks past Emil, sighing painfully with tears filling his eyes, as he avoids looking at his best friend's dead body. Xena frowns and hugs him for a quick moment before he walks off. Christopher looks ready to toss his lunch but swallows. Likewise with Richard. I shake it off and head back over to the coffee table and pick up one of the cards. I read and divide the stack into two groups with five cards in each.

"Zoe," Xena calls as Zoe runs over to me, angry.

"Why are you messing with the cards at a time like this? Emil just died," Zoe yells, pushing all the cards off the table.

I pick the cards up off the floor.

"Emil just died, and all you are thinking about is this stupid game," she cries pushing me on the ground.

Taking a deep breath, ignoring it, I get off the floor and continue picking the cards up. She stares at me with an angry look, but I place the cards back on the table to sort them.

While sorting them she kicks me in my side, causing me to fall to the ground again. I feel a sharp pain.

"Zoe, stop!" Christopher yells, "Emil knew what he was getting himself into."

"Maybe not exactly but…" Xena stops talking. "He knew what would be happening tonight."

Xena comes over to help me off the ground while Zoe charges at me as I get to my feet. Xena moves out of the way.

In a quick motion, I punch her stomach and place her in a chokehold. No one seems shocked.

I am upset at Zoe but all I want to do is get this game over with. Her face starts to turn bright red as she is gasping for air.

The smell of Emil's dead body fills the room.

"One thing you will not do is touch me or blame me for what just happened to Emil. You are a part of my group, so you better behave unless you want to end up like him," I threaten.

Xena looks at me, then motions her head no while pushing her eyebrows in. I assume that she's saying what I'm doing is a waste of time. I roll my eyes in anger.

Then whisper, "And I'd be willing to help you see him again."

Letting her go, I split up the cards again.

"Um, so…how do you know that she is in your group?" Deondra asks, walking out back into the dorm with Mark.

"When we were thrown into the wall I was on one side of the room with Christopher and Zoe…and Emil, while the rest of you were on the other. I'm assuming that those are the groups," I respond.

"What does the card in your hand say?" Richard asks, pointing at it.

My eyes can't help but glance into his eyes as his lips let out a small, yet obvious, smile.

"Well, before Zoe messed up the order…" I glare at her. "…the card told me to make two groups of five. For each team."

"I'm not sorry," Zoe laughs.

"You will be if you die," I grin, handing Richard one of the stacks of five cards.

She swallows hard, placing distance between us.
Taking a quick glance at Emil's dead body, while wiping away her tears.
The lights then cut off.
It goes quiet.
I feel a light breeze brush past me.

"One thing to remember is that these two groups are not enemies with each other. We are trying to beat this creature. As long as two people, someone and myself, make it to the end before sunrise, we win and the game is over," I whisper as the dorm lights turn green.

Odd enough, I take that as the sign that we are okay to start.
So we split into our groups and worked with our stack of cards.
I put the cards in a line together like solving a puzzle. It took Zoe, Christopher, and I a couple of minutes to solve it, but we finally got it.
It reads:

Many have tried, none have succeeded.
Trade this note in a place for exercise but don't be fooled by how much we lift.
If you care at all, don't drink the love potion.

"That must be the gym," Zoe exclaims with excitement.
Running out of the dorm.
Christopher and I shrug and run out of the door room after her. I tie my jacket around my waist, feeling a slight sting on my side.
The hallway is quiet, and the lights are dim. My heart is beating fast as Zoe's non-stop talking echoes around us. She must be trying to distract herself from thinking about Emil's death or thinking about how we all could die in general. Real-life horror movie.
I understand that it's hard to sit here and continue going when we all just watched a man die, but it's out of my control. Or any of ours for that matter.
The college is four stories high. According to the map, the gym is on the west wing. So we run down two flights of stairs to get to the main floor. Wheezing by the time we get to the bottom.
It is six o'clock and the sun hasn't set yet, but even then, no one in the hallway.

It is like we are either in a whole new world or everyone not in this game disappeared.

Pairings {Xena}

Richard and I put the cards together and read the riddle out loud:

"The key is with the children
But you must show me your skills first."

He then runs out of the dorm unit and the three of us quickly follow behind him. Regardless of the reason your group runs, everyone needs to run. It's called sticking together and not dying.

Lowell's group is still in the dorm when we leave. They look like they are struggling but they didn't want our help when asked.

The hallway is quiet, like state testing, and all the doors are closed on the third floor.

Richard and I walk closer to the wall farthest from the rails on the other side of this verandah hallway. It wraps around all floors of the college and acts as an outside hallway.

Anyway, we got paired with the best, I think sarcastically, glancing at Richard and then the couple. Deondra and Mark are walking slower behind us and are doing annoying couple stuff as we try to solve the riddle.

"When it comes to children, I assume that it would be kids younger than us…but this college has no daycare center. Also the 'showing your skills part' doesn't make sense," I say to Richard as he reads the card over again.

He looks so focused when he reads.

His eyebrows go in. My face gets softer. His eyes feel welcoming… I bite my lip-

"What if it's saying that we need to go to a place where there are or would be a lot of kids? Open mic night would have tons of kids and bring out writing/speech skills among them. Maybe we have to go to the show and perform in order to find the next clue."

Excitement spreads across his face as I am amazed by how quickly he solved that. It does make sense and of course, I trust his judgment. However, I know that he probably drew that conclusion because of how badly he wanted to perform.

I smile, nudging him.

We silently walk down the hallway making our way to the west wing. It comes as a surprise that no one else is walking on the third floor, and the sun is still out. If this was any other type of situation, it would be nice to take a break and figure out why this life-or-death game is happening. However, I can't voice my opinions because Richard is too focused. Our partners, Deondra and Mark, disappeared while Richard and I were talking.

Hopefully, they will come back soon. That is, if we don't find them dead.

The sun pours against the hallway walls, and I look over the rail to see if anyone is outside. Outside being the campus lawn. But just like the hallways, no one is there.

Looking at my phone to see what time it is, it stays off.

"Out cold" is what my mom says, but it's just dead.

"Richard, do you know what time it is? My phone's out cold. But I swear it was on eighty-five percent before we started."

"I don't know. My phone is dead too, but that's just because I forgot to charge it."

He then pauses and looks around the hallway.

"Umm…if you want to make a pit stop, there is a huge clock in the library we can look at," he responds.

I shrug, then nod my head yes.

We start running towards the stairs on the west wing and go down one flight. The second floor has poetry hanging on the walls and artistic designs, from a previous art project my classmates and I were required to do, replacing most of the basic white ceiling.

Hallway lights above us flicker but it is pitch black in the distance.

I begin to drag my left hand along the wall to calm myself down. It relieves some of the shaking that occurs when my fears start creeping up on me.

Though my shaking gets worse.

The library is in the direction of the darkness. Scared, Richard and I creep towards it.

We stop under the last light that is on and stare into the dark part of the hallway. After a while of just standing there staring, I see two red dots in the darkness. I gasp as I hear a crashing noise from inside. It goes quiet.

Richard and I then looked at each other, as if it was a debate on whether we would go and investigate. Nodding our heads at each other, we turn around, sprinting back up the stairs. It was like we were never there to begin with.

Catching our breaths, we start jogging and look around.

I quickly glance behind us to make sure nothing is following. Reassuring our safety as we decide to slow our pace to a walk again.

It is bright in this hallway. The sun is still shining, unlike the second floor. Though something about the math class I am taking on this third floor is calling my name. So, I duck inside.

Richard follows and closes the door behind us.

The classroom lights aren't working, and the desks are in straight rows and columns. Looks better now than it did when I showed up to get my summer math work.

Silence except for our fast breathing fills the room.

I start looking around for a flashlight in the drawer. My fingers wrap around one, so I pull on Richard's backpack to put it in there.

We then start softly laughing because of what just happened with the red dots. My eyes wander to the clock on the wall.

"It's 5:50," I raise my eyebrow, confused, pointing at the clock.

I thought I'd be 6 by now.

He smiles back at me and shrugs. His smile is faint yet obvious to see.

"We have to think of something because we can't just wait out the next two hours. The open mic doesn't start until 8," I announce.

"Well, what if performance is not the skill we have to perform? What if the skill is how well we can find something? Like hide and seek!" he exclaims.

"That's smart and actually makes sense. A treasure-hunting game is just a series of finding and solving puzzles anyway. How are you so good at this?"

"I guess my skill would be solving riddles, so without me, this would be a disaster for you," he teases.

"Well, in that case…I'm glad you didn't try to investigate those two red dots."

"Yeah, no, we don't investigate. Either the creature finds and kills us first or we flee the scene in the beginning," he laughs.

Referring to black people in horror movies.

"Then we might as well get going before it does find us," I add, walking over to the door.

"Wait...c-can I make a statement first?" He stutters.

"Yeah. You don't have to ask."

He looks down at me. With an empty expression on his face and thoughts on his mind. Every time he does this, he always looks at me like I'm the only person in the world.

"Well…I'm glad you and I are in the same college. I missed the last two years of your life, and I'm sorry for everything I put you through during high school."

"The past is in the past. All that matters is that you're here now, and…I guess I missed you too," I sigh deeply.

His warm hands intertwined with mine as we smile at each other. My heart races faster as he stares into my soul.

"Thank you for being so understanding. And for never thinking I killed those kids," he frowns.

I glance away.

"Honestly, it did cross my mind once, but I think playing this game makes me understand that you didn't do it. Besides, I was more upset that you wouldn't let me celebrate your 15th birthday with you."

Inhaling sharply, he then swallows hard and looks away from me.

"That was because I just met you. We hit it off perfectly for months and…" He pauses as I move his head gently by his chin.

Making deep eye contact.

"I get it," I say softly.

His eyes stare into my soul, causing my face to get heated.

"I didn't want there to be any possibility of losing you," he replies with a faint smile.

"So instead, you decided to leave me alone and never come back…you do that often."

A frown then spreads slightly across both our faces as I look back at the exit. His love for me hurts sometimes but I don't blame him. He only knows toxic love and absence. His parents raised him under those ideas and actions, even if they didn't know it. Though Richard has been working on himself. He's not the same man he used to be, and I'm happy for him.

I then slowly open the door, just as we hear something fall in the storage closet of the classroom. It was a loud metal clang that reminded me of dropping a pot on the kitchen floor.

Fear courses through my veins as the closest door slowly creaks open. A scary scene from any horror movie just before the person dies.

Richard and I glance at each other and dart out of the door.

Closing it behind us. As we take long strides from it, something throws the door open. It hits the wall hard.

Continuing to sprint down the hallway, a voice behind us shouts "DON'T LEAVE!" while coughing hard.

We are getting closer and closer to another door in the hallway that we end up running past, but out of nowhere, Richard grabs my waist and pulls me back into the open mic performance room after we had just passed the door.

He then locks it behind us.

Footsteps lingering outside the door cause us to remain quiet.

He tries catching his breath as I walk around the room.

It is huge, with walls that are painted ombre orange. The darker orange being on the roof of the wall.

Along with beautiful walls, high stools and tables scatter the room, and a microphone sits in the center of the stage.

The room gives a vintage bar appearance, and I favor the festoon lights hanging from the ceiling.

Richard admires himself in the mirror as I run my hand against the wall. It feels smooth overall, but one section close to the floor is rough. My face lights up as I call Richard over.

He helps me move the chairs out of the way so we can get more space. We knock on the wall but hear nothing back.

"Bingo!" I exclaim, smiling.

He then digs through his backpack and pulls out a small hammer. Breaking the wall in, he pulls out an item. There is a note on top of a small, padlocked chest.

He hands me the chest as he reads the note aloud.

I am simple to please if you can help me
Keep the chest, find the key
~~*Then release me*~~

That sounds more like a message than a location," I announce, leaning my back against the wall.

"It is a message but look at the back. This note is for you," his voice shakes.

"What do you mean?"

I grab the note, flipping it over:

You remind me of someone close to me
If only they still lived in C333

"Richard, I don't like this game. How is this treasure hunting?" I say, stuffing the note in my pocket.

"Well, the goal of the game is to follow all the riddles until you find the prize at the end. The only issue would be that the game is manipulated so you can't win. The clues are harder, people disappear, and just when you think that you have made it to the end…he throws in a curveball," Richard replies, in a spooky announcer voice.

"He?"

"Yes."

His eyes make his fear obvious to the public, while his face stays cold. I grab his hand and help him up. Holding them until he makes eye contact with me. I've never seen him scared before.

"Let's go find the key," I nod, terrified on the inside.

We then unlock the door, look both ways, and run toward our dorm unit at a normal pace. The hallway is now darker than when we first ran up here.

We turn into the moonlit hallway and see that the ceiling is covered in blood. Richard and I walk in the middle of the hallway, past the C100 and C200 dorm units. When we approach our dorm unit door, I feel a wet substance under my feet.

Looking down, it is blood. Coming from under the door.

I don't scream or say anything to Richard as I touch his shoulder. Pointing at the blood. We look back and forth at each other, trying to figure out who was going to enter the room first or guessing whose blood it could belong to. But he rolls his eyes halfway through the glances.

He opens the door, and we slowly walk through it. The smell of death filling our noses like earlier when Emil suffered a terrible death.

I don't want to be in here, I think to myself while glancing at the easel. Emil is still dead.

Lifeless and cold.

I don't stop looking at him as if he would randomly get up and try to kill us.

The room lights are off as we slowly creep inside. All of a sudden it feels cooler as goosebumps form on my skin.

The door loudly closed behind us. We both jump. Causing me to quickly grab Richard's hand.

My heart races fast. We freeze in place as something hovers behind us. Blood dripping on my shoulder. Nervous, and feeling like this is a stupid idea, we turn around to see who closed the door, and there it was. The shadow figure towering above us, as we slowly sneak backward.

I stare at the figure in his eyes and feel for a light switch on the wall. He steps forward and I flick one on.

He disappears.

We both sigh and keep walking backward faster.

Assuming that we were just seeing things, I turn around and notice that the three had fallen off my dorm wall. Richard keeps facing the direction of where we saw the creature in case it comes back.

Quickly. I pull my key out of my pocket and grab the knob. My hands aggressively shake as I accidentally twist the knob.

Is it already unlocked?

I start hyperventilating as my hand continues shaking against the door. Richard looks at me, putting a hand on my shoulder. That's when we feel this light breeze brush past us. Richard and I simultaneously look in the direction of the lounge and I cut the lights off. The shadow is standing closer to us holding something. I gasp quietly, feeling my heart stop for a moment.

Scared, Richard puts his arm over me to block me while I stand behind him. It is quiet but I can hear my heart beating out of my chest. Mark then walks towards us.

"Sorry if I scared you guys. Deondra and I didn't mean to leave you two alone," he chuckles.

Ironically, he is unknowingly standing in front of the shadow. Richard then slowly opens the door as I slowly point behind Mark. The shadow raises his arms above Mark but Mark just stands there talking about Deondra.

"What are you pointing at?" he questioned, cutting his flashlight on.

As he turned around and shined the flashlight on the creature's face, that part of him disappeared. His eyes go wide. He screams. Quickly pushing his way into my room. His pushing causes Richard to fall on top of me. Mark then locks the door and sits on Deondra's bed, trying to calm himself down.

I lay on the floor. My face is red from pain and fear.

Richard lays on top of me with his hands placed by my ears from the fall. His face turns tomato red against his brown skin as we look into each other's eyes.

My heart races faster when he places his hand on my face and relaxes his body. He holds each other in our eyes, and we glance down at each other's lips. Before looking at each other again. I touch his face as I think, *I know you feel it too.* Our faces moving closer and closer to each other.

"What was that?" Mark shudders in fear.

His sudden speaking breaks the tension and knocks Richard and me back to reality. Richard then helps me up off the ground as we make distance between each other. Nervously laughing.

I pull the notes out of my pocket and look around the room to see what they mean.

"That was the creature…or at least I think it was," Richard whispers.

I ignore the rest of the conversation Mark and Richard are having while I search the room. Cutting on the room lights and reading the notes over again. I knock on the wall to see if any spots are different, but I find nothing. My eyes then wander to Richard's right hand as he stands in front of Mark.

It is covered in blood.

"Richard, you're hurt!"

If Trees Could Talk {Lowell}

It is about 7:00, and we still haven't solved the riddle. We circled the gym three times for thirty minutes or so looking for a clue, and we still have nothing.

The sun is still out. Though it will set in about an hour. Once night falls, it will be harder to solve these riddles, since the lights in the university aren't working properly.

It'll be darker, so the shadow will be able to pick us off easier.

Earlier, while we were looking around, we saw the creature lingering in the hallway, so we had to detour before coming to the gym. Dragged Zoe's slow self inside. We locked the door behind us at that time. At some point we heard scratching on the other side, so we decided not to walk near the door at all in case it could ~~hear~~ see us.

"AHHHH!!!" Zoe screams, halting in the middle of the gym.

Christopher and I jump at first and stop looking around. Walking over to see what is wrong with Zoe.

"Are you feeling well?" Christopher asks.

"I'm sweating," she cries, jumping up and down, waving her arms.

I want to slap her. But with Xena in mind, I decide not to waste my energy on someone so pathetic. So I just roll my eyes along with Christopher and read the card again.

Many have tried but none have succeeded.
Trade this in a place for exercise but don't be fooled by how much we lift.
If you care at all, don't drink the love potion

The words "If you care at all, don't drink the love potion" stand out the most to me.

While standing in the middle of the gym, I think about how people can fall in love here. Weights, treadmills, and ellipticals are knocked down across the room due to us looking around, the aroma of sweat and musk makes my eyes water to the point of almost throwing up, and most women fear coming here, for some men can be perverts and make us uncomfortable.

"I don't understand the clue. How does someone fall in love here?" I whine, sitting on the floor.

"Maybe this isn't the room," Zoe says, pulling out her phone.

"How much battery do you have?" Christopher asks.

"Fifty percent. Why?"

"Can you text Richard and ask him what the riddle means? Someone in the group might know."

"Actually, just text all four of them, just in case their phones have died," I add.

"Fine. You're so needy. I'll send this through the group chat," Zoe says, rolling her eyes. "Should have just taken their help from the beginning."

Texting them.

As we wait for one of them to respond, Christopher and I sit and reread the card multiple times. While waiting for Zoe to receive a text, my eyes can't help but be distracted by her constant pacing around.

"Mark texted back. He said that Richard said that it is the dance room. Mark also said that both Xena and Richard put their dead phones on the charger."

"Did he explain why?" I ask, standing up.

"Because their phone is dead," she laughs, shaking her head at me.

"No, did they explain why it's the dance room, Zoe?" I clarify, annoyed.

"It doesn't matter, let's just go."

"Zoe," Christopher shoots - his eyes glare sharply. "We don't want to keep running around the college. His thought process could help."

"Fine," she whines, looking back at the phone. "He said that due to dancers being so close to each other there is a possibility of catching feelings in some cases. Also, something about you being muscular surprised him. Especially when he found out you were a dancer, Christopher."

"He remembered?" Christopher whispers to himself just as I say, "Don't be fooled by how much we lift. It makes sense, ya know. Dancers lift people."

"Yes, okay, yes, now let's go. I'm tired of being in this sweaty gym."

Excited, we run out of the gym following Christopher as he leads the way.

While running, we look at the stairs and realize that we have to go up four flights. The dance room is on the fourth floor.

The circular stairs with a central landing on every floor make it feel like a long way up. Zoe suggests that we use the elevator, but with the current electricity problem, we might not survive an elevator ride.

When we finally make it to the fourth floor, Christopher is carrying Zoe on his back. She had jumped on his back once we passed the second floor.

"You know Christopher, your jawline is really sharp. Like it could CUT me," she teases, poking his face.

He then rolls his eyes and drops her on the floor. My laughter echoes through the hall as she looks at me in anger. I stick my tongue out at her.

"Owww. Why did you do that? I could have broken a nail!"

"Shhh," I say, covering her mouth.

I let go and stare into the hallway.

The walls are filled with pictures of dancers and posters of acting performances the theatre kids put on over the years. Colorful streamers hang from the ceiling too, as a huge red carpet runs through the middle of the floor. Christopher is in one holding a girl which I suspect is from last years' Christmas show he invited me too.

We follow it to the theatre and close the door behind us.

Proceeding to walk down the aisle, passing the velvet seats for the audience, towards the stage. Christopher guides us backstage and through the door of the major dance room.

There is a huge mirror on the wall and a small wooden stage on the floor with a heart in the middle. A long ballet pole wrapped around the wall of the room.

It is dim in here, yet beautiful. Kinda scary too but that's mostly because slow music is playing while no one else is in here.

After being amazed by the room, we start looking for clues.

I go into the women's changing room filled with lockers. Zoe, who I did not want to be on my team, follows me and slams every single locker I open, shut. Try my best to ignore her and we leave to go to the male's changing room to check for clues. She just keeps following me.

"Lalalalalalala," Zoe sings off-key.

I just continue ignoring her and walk back into the room with Christopher. We look under the pictures on the wall, and under the carpet, as Zoe jumps in the middle of the stage singing.

"LALALALA AAAAAAHHHHHH," she yells off key.

"Can you please shut up?" I beg as she jumps around.

"NO NO NO NOOOOOO," she sings.

She's not worried that we could die, and her making noise might just attract the creature to us.

She wouldn't stop making my ears bleed.

After a while of making us listen to her tone-deaf singing, she slips and falls. I start laughing so hard that I start to cry. Christopher joins in.

She slipped on the heart in the middle of the floor. With the sliding and jumping she was doing, it simply moved under her. For it to move that easily is a safety hazard in a dance room where turns, jumps and stomping is most promised against the floor.

Wiping away my tears as mine and Christopher's laughter slowly stops, Zoe gets up.

It must have been her sudden movement because the floor is now starting to cave in.

I run over to hug the side walls.

A huge, gaping hole forms around the small piece of floor Zoe is standing around. Scared tears run down her face as parts of the floor under her drop. Every time she moves, more falls. *She's going to die if she doesn't stand still,* I think to myself as I glare into the hole. It is dark. Dropping something inside is like dropping something into a 7ft well.

"Hey, look at me," I say in a soothing voice as Zoe makes eye contact.

Inching closer to her, without falling in the hole, I hold my hands out. Christopher then points out that there is a riddle in the hole taped along the wall. He inches closer to that. I continue to make sure Zoe is okay.

"No, don't look at him. Look at me." I tell Zoe again.

The floor is slowly dropping under her feet.

"You're going to have to jump, okay?"

"No…no, I can't. You will drop me, I may slip, I'm too heavy, especially since I had that muffin earlier and-"

"Zoe, please shut up," Christopher adds.

She looks at him, then back at me.

"Trust me. I won't drop you," I say, nodding my head to comfort her.

Even though my brain is telling me *"you can't catch"* which is true. I also have no balance and a low reaction time.. But I can't say that to her or psych myself out.

Zoe then takes a deep breath, and with a sliver of the floor left, she falls forward with stretched out arms. The most petite jump ever. I quickly scramble forward and grab both of her elbows. *"Fuck she's heavy!"*

She screams "Pull me up!" repeatedly as I pull her up by her belt. Causing me to fall backward.

She looks at me with a smile. Our faces nearly inches apart as she sits on top of me. Makes me feel uncomfortable so I push her off.

"Ouch, you meanie." she pouts.

Landing on her butt.

"Sorry!" I say, touching her shoulder softly.

She smiles faintly, rolling her eyes.

Then, the sound of something crashing catches our attention. Zoe and I stare at the hole as it caves in. Christopher quickly sticks his hand inside just before it completely closes on him. He pulls out a card and shows it to us while breathing heavy. All of us are trying to calm our nerves and fast-beating hearts.

It reads:

Don't just think about why you are here
Conquer your fears or tell the truth
You have until sunrise

When I finish reading it, I let out a bellow of rage. Lying on the ground.

"Calm down, Lowell. We still have 11 hours to finish this," Christopher reassures. Handing me the card.

"This one isn't even a riddle, it's a task."

I sit up and look at Zoe. As she is now walking around scrolling through her phone.

All of a sudden, the music speed picks up and the lights cut off. Zoe lets out a quick high-pitched scream. Causing me to drop the card.

Getting onto my knees, I try feeling around for the card.

When I find it, I put it in my pocket. We all remain still for one minute as to assess what to do next. Whispering to see if anyone was near me. Christopher answers.

He grabs my hand, as we crawl around looking for Zoe.

It then sounds like he whispers, "I have to use the bathroom," but I can barely hear.

"Terrible timing," I think, *"I don't want to be left alone."*

The music proceeds to get louder and Christopher lets go of my hand. He runs into the men's changing room, and the lights turn blue. That's when I see Zoe on the other side of the room.

She runs over towards me smiling like a weirdo. She then jumps into my arms and kisses my cheek. I push her off me hard, wiping off my cheek. She laughs softly. Disgusting. She then lays her head on my shoulder. Maybe she is scared or maybe she is high. Her eyes red.

We sit there in silence for a while as the lights remain blue.

"What's your biggest fear?" I ask Zoe.

It takes everything inside of me to not push her off my shoulder. Why is she trying to cuddle with me at a scary time like this? We can barely tolerate each other. What's up with her? Maybe she is high… I should have smoked whatever she's on.

"It was telling Emil that I like him. Though…that fear is dead now, along with him," she replies, tears in her eyes.

The lights then turn green and go right back to blue.

"It's fine, though. If I pass away then at least I'll see him again, as you said."

"I'm sorry for your loss!" I say, as she glances at me. "I didn't know anything about him, but he seems like an amazing person nonetheless."

"Didn't know you had a heart…" she laughs painfully. "But I don't need your sympathy."

"It's the game Zoe… I can't control anything done."

She nods. Sighing.

"I know you don't actually care, but he was amazing. He loved photography," she faintly smiles. "I carry our photo all the time," she says, showing me.

It's an image of her standing on the edge of a bridge as if she is about to jump. Her blonde hair is covering up half her face. Emil is holding her hand right next to her. Both of them soaked in the rain.

"What does it represent?"

"It means that we will jump together if it's our time. Face our fears together. I know jumping off a bridge is terrible, and I don't recommend doing it, but the image represents that we aren't fighting our battles alone. So, when I feel alone I just think about the image and how much fun that depressing day was. How he…saved me," she faintly smiles, putting it back in her bra.

"Oh," I sigh.

Feeling bad for her.

She's on her cycle and lost her friend. It's hard.

"I'm sorry for nearly choking you out earlier!"

"I won't accept that apology. And I don't expect you to accept mine. I accidentally did cut you on the side after kicking you. So, we're even."

"Oh."

"Yeah," she smiles.

Out of the corner of my eye, I see Christopher walking out of the dressing room. He sits down with us.

"Why did you run into the changing room?"

"I told Lowell I had to use the bathroom."

"That's a good mentality. Don't want to have pee in your pants when you die," she jokes, nodding her head.

I shrug and nod my head *"true"* as she smiles at him through a pained look.

"So, what is your biggest fear?" Zoe asks.

"Wolves. And spiders."

Zoe snickers, covering her mouth after she lets out a loud snort. We all then burst into laughter as the light above turns green. It stays that way for a minute before going back to blue.

I feel like the blue light means that the creature is waiting on us and green means correct and/or go.

I stand up and walk over to the door. It's locked.

"You said I have until sunrise," I announce as the lights turn green.

A card then drops from the ceiling and I jump, scared, as it hits my head.

The key is in a tree
But don't leave

The others walk over to me, and we realize that the sun is already setting. Time goes by a lot quicker than it feels like, but I'm optimistic about winning this game.

I flip the card over to see if there is anything on the back. Surprisingly, there is. It reads:

Now the fun starts

With a smiley face drawing at the end.

Christopher and I shrug, walking out of the room first. The door then closes just as Zoe tries to leave.

Locking her inside.

She bangs on the other side of the door as we try to open it. She screams and cries on the other side, but the door is locked. Then she goes quiet.

Blood runs under the door, touching both Christopher's and my feet. We stare in shock as a light smell of death, like rotting food, fills my nose. Backing up, the door swings open and we see Zoe laying on the floor. Blood pours out of her, but she is still breathing.

Christopher quickly picks her up, bridal style, as we head to the clinic as fast as we can. Trying to leave the dance area before anything else happens. Her blood drops on the floor leaving a trail behind us.

We go down four flights of stairs to the main floor. The floor, just like the others, is quiet, and the sky is completely dark. With stars and everything. Zoe, being the strong woman she is, is breathing, even though blood is pouring out of her head. She seemed to be just injured like she cracked her head open. Yet not in too bad shape.

Even though cracking your head is a deep wound.

"Wait…d-don't leave," a voice yells, in a broken tone from behind us.

Breathing hard.

I turn around as Christopher walks into the clinic. "Deondra?" I think to myself, wondering why she is alone. She is bleeding from her side, so I run over and help her get into the clinic. I then lock the door. She sits on one of the beds. Zoe on the other bed.

"Why are you alone?"

"Well, **cough** Mark and I decided to leave the others and go back to the dorms to have fun. We were doing **cough** couples' stuff when **cough** I heard a knock on the door. I opened it and I was **cough** sliced in the stomach. I laid there **cough** bleeding **cough** as Mark ran to get help. He never came back," she cried through struggled speech.

The more comfortable she got on the bed, the more her blood dripped off the sides through bandages she must have tied herself. She looks tired, so I drape the blanket I got from the closet over her. She is losing so much blood that wrapping it again wouldn't save her life either way.

"Deondra, don't close your eyes. Please stay with me."

"I don't regret playing this game. I know you will win," she whispers, coughing up blood.

Zoe tries not to look but she cries a little.

Deondra's eyes then close. They never reopen.

My eyes tear up as I cover her face in the blanket and walk over to Christopher. He had wrapped Zoe's head with bandages and gave her water to drink.

She sits on the bed drinking water and crying at the loss of not just her future boyfriend from earlier, but now her best friend.

"What happened in there?" I ask her.

"I was hit in the head… twisted my ankle and fall to the floor, I probably… died. Yes, almost died. Something was shooting at me from the distance," she stutters, swallowing hard.

Her speech making no since I'm staring to think she hit her head a little harder than she might notice.

Her body is shaking, and her ankle looks like it did more than twist. Like on top of twisting it did a whole somersault, backflip.

I want to throw up at the sight of it bleeding and swelling like it is about to explode.

But I just look around the clinic for extra medical supplies to help her.

The cabinets are filled with cotton balls, tissue, and bandages. The fridge is filled with soda, water, and someone's lunch. I brought another water bottle to Zoe, so she wouldn't have to move later, and gave her some extra bandages. She held them in her hands, staring at me. I then pull the card from earlier out of my pocket and hand it to Christopher.

She's acting like she can't even feel the pain in her ankle.

"We need to go to the campus lawn. The key must be in one of those trees," I say as he helps Zoe off of the bed. I then add with a whisper, "We need to go by ourselves. Zoe is only going to slow us down," as he looks at me, shocked.

He lets go of Zoe and pulls me to the side. She sits on the bed in silence.

"Not taking her makes sense, but what if she gets taken while we are gone?"

"What if we all get taken while she is with us? She'll slow us down. You know that once I die the game is over and we all die."

I looked at her.

She was on her phone, enjoying life and wincing here and there with tears in her eyes.

"Guys, I can stay here by myself. As long as I lock the door, I will be fine," she says, rolling her eyes at our bickering.

"Just stay safe," I say, as Christopher walks out of the door.

I am stressed out. And my side is finally feeling some real sharp pain.

I run after Christopher as he walks down the split staircase leading to the lawn. The lawn is huge and there are two trees. The one on the left is red and the one on the right is green.

The moonlight shines away from the trees as stars scatter across the night sky. Standing next to Christopher, he contemplates out loud which tree we should go to first.

"We should go to the green tree," I suggest.

"Then you go to the green tree. I will go to the red one."

"We will get killed if we split up. That's how it always goes in scary movies, so why do that now?"

"You seem to have no problem with wanting to leave people."

"Christopher…"

"We will find the key quicker, and besides, we haven't solved a riddle yet on our own," he snaps.

"Do you need to get something off your chest? Because you're being a pain in the ass right now."

My face goes cold as Christopher rolls his eyes and walks away to the red tree.

I follow behind him so we don't die. Walking next to him across the lawn as he remains quiet.

It is dark. We have no flashlights, so we must rely on the lights from the university building to see. Which is little to none based on how far we are.

I stand under the tree and look up.

It's huge. The leaves are beautiful from what I can see.

Christopher still isn't talking to me. He looks around the tree. I climb it to search through the leaves but find nothing except the beautiful smell of nature and a warm temperature. While I am sitting at the top of the tree, feeling utmost peace, Christopher walks away towards the green tree.

I slowly climb down and run after him when my feet are safely on the ground.

When we make it to the green tree across the lawn, he begins to search through it. We don't dig up the ground, but I do climb this tree just like I did with the last one. The smell over here is different and the temperature is rather cold as to mimic citrus by a campfire.

When I get up to the top of the tree, I search through the leaves.

That's when I see a card taped to a branch. I wave Christopher over to me as he rolls his eyes before coming. He stands under the tree staring at me before we see something charging at us from a distance. I squint. It looks like an animal, but it is bigger than any I've ever seen. It's getting closer. Its teeth are sharp. Two more follow behind.

"Climb!" I yell as he jumps up.

I grab his hands as he uses his feet to help him up. He's heavy, but I manage to pull him up just as the animals bite at his feet. Wolves are what they look like up close.

They were common in this town until hunters made them go extinct…years ago. But of course, they are back and bigger than ever, just when I was at peace in this fearful game.

Christopher sits next to me as the wolves snap at us.

I wince, relaxing my leg. Christopher's eyes are fearful as he can't take his eyes off the wolves. They are pacing around the tree, so we stay put. Waiting for them to fall asleep or leave.

I grab the card off the branch and read it aloud.

We have time to think about what this means:

If you make it out alive
Then jump in the water
And take a dive

"Wow. We finally get an easy one and we have to wait," Christopher says.

I look at him with a confused expression as he rolls his eyes.

"It's the swimming pool next to the west wing," he adds, annoyed, looking away from me.

"Oh, well, when we get down from here then that will be the first place we go."

Silence.

He continues to stare in the opposite direction from me.

Usually, he comforts me when times get hard, so I've never seen him this way. He snapped on me earlier, left me in the last tree, and ignored most of what I said.

I lean against one of the branches to stay comfortable since it is cramped. Christopher's and my feet are intertwined due to it being such a small space for our long legs. It hurts slightly, so I reposition my body. Sitting more on my right waist. Staring at the wolves, they continue to circle the tree. Two more come around to join them.

"I hope that we won't be up here for that long," he announces out of the blue.

"Why? Are you tired of being in the same group as me?"

"That is not what my statement meant."

"Then why are you acting so different? You're usually so calm and reassuring but you seem so sad right now. Why is that?" I argue.

He goes silent, breaking eye contact with me. His eyes fill with tears but he doesn't cry. I roll my eyes.

"Okay, fine. I'm not going to force you so just tell me whenever you feel comfortable enough," I shrug, placing my hand on my chest.

I'm tired.

His eyes fill with tears, as a couple of teardrops slide down his face.

"May I?" I ask, pointing at his face.

He just shrugs, so I proceed to wipe them away as he grabs my hand. More tears fall down his face and my heart starts to throb.

"I was 9…during my golden birthday, a-and my friends agreed to play a game of chess with me. Six players playing a life-size version. That's what the creature did to my game. It made it…real. To make a long story short, we won, and since we won, everything went back to normal the next day."

He pauses, then continues.

I continue to look engaged at his rapid speaking and lack of hand motions.

"No one was dead anymore but for a couple of months, I received multiple emails and notes from my friends. They said things about how I should have died, that they hate me, and why they never liked me. I failed to know if it was because of the game or if it was their honest opinion, so I chose both. I remember going to school one day, and they were standing at the entrance doors. I tried to walk past them but they beat me up. Cut at my body until my pool of blood stained the sidewalk. They left me there. Teachers didn't even come to help, they just walked past me. I laid there for hours until my parents came to the school because I missed the bus. I was hospitalized for a week and when I went back to school I was an outcast. Everyone I once knew said that if I ever wanted people to like me then I should change my personality and be nicer…. but I tried and still couldn't get people to like me. In the end, I separated myself and choose not to have any friends. Every time I get sad, angry, or defensive, people leave my life. People assume that I can't do something or act a certain way because I prefer to smile at life and…cry alone," his voice breaks.

"I'm sorry!"

Speechless, I hug him.

His body tenses up and he looks away from me. Tears fall harder, so I move off and place his hands in mine.

"Hey, just know you're not alone. I have a fear of staying in a relationship and being with someone that can actually, truly love me because I've been receiving fake love my whole life. So my emotions are locked up too," I say.

A random light on campus then turns green.

Christopher smiles through tears.

His icy blue eyes look faded, like the happiness in his heart.

"You suck at pep talks. And being emotional," he laughs, pulling me in close.

We sit like that for a while.

In silence as the wolves snore below us.

Even though neither I nor Christopher have our phones, it felt like hours had gone by. Hours of hugging each other in peace as he rested his eyes while laying his head on my shoulder.

I sigh.

A vivid memory of my father drinking every night, and my mom coming home to put out her cigarettes on my legs as he beats on her, runs through my head. All I could do was pretend it didn't hurt while my sister was praised as the golden child and left untouched.

Tears fill my eyes. I sigh again, leaning my head against the tree. Looking up at the dark sky.

I suck at all of this because no one knows that I'm used to seeing the bad. If you don't get attached, then you won't get hurt.

Poisoned Promises {Xena}

I grab his hand, inspecting the blood.

"Xena, I'm fine. It's not even my blood."

He then turns around, looking at Mark. His arms and shirt are covered in blood.

"Mark, you know that there is blood covering your torso, right? Do you have any injuries? Your arms look like they are in pain," I question, as he looks down.

His eyes start to water but he just clears his throat. A way to stop himself from choking up.

"No, most of this is Deondra's blood… some of it could be mine. I wouldn't know," he lamented, staring at the floor.

"Where is Deondra?" Richard asks.

"I don't know. I left the dorm to find help after she was cut on her side, but when I came back…she was gone."

Mark then gets off the bed and sits next to the door. I don't want to tell Mark that she is probably dead, so I continue to look for the key. Richard looks around also. He tries to move Deondra's bed as I did the same with mine. But we see that it's bolted to the floor. Shortly after, we realized it wouldn't budge.

I stare around the room. Scanning the ceiling as I get distracted, I realize that the painting on the wall was here before me. It is a picture of a girl in a white dress holding a guy's hand. There is a gaping hole over him so I can't see what they looked like in the face.

As I stare at the painting, I notice that the roof starts to grow higher. We must have to get the picture frame since it's the only thing purposefully distancing itself.

While standing up on the edge of my bed reaching for the painting, the roof stops raising itself. The painting is on the ceiling above the closet, which is three feet away from the end of my bed.

I know I'm still too short, but I stand on my tippy toes and reach for the painting anyway. Like I'm magically gonna start growing too.

"You need help?" Richard offers, standing under me.

I shrug. "Yes, please."

He holds his arms out, standing directly under me on the floor. I grab his shoulders as he places his hands on my waist. Trying not to laugh, I slide my leg on his shoulder and sit down.

Assuming that the wall was 8 feet before it grew, it looks like it it's 14 feet now. Continuing to reach, my arms get tired so I fully sit down on Richard's shoulders.

"Richard, how tall are you?" I ask in a soft voice, looking down into his eyes.

His face gets closer to mine as my body relaxes. I can tell he is turning red, as he lays the back of his head against my stomach. His hands gripping my thighs for support reminding me of how he used to grip me. Still just as soft as to not "break me." I try not to get flustered as he looks back up at me with doe eyes. A smile across my face as one of my hands accidentally starts playing with his beautiful short dreads. The other sits on his defined jawline.

I must not pay much attention to him much anymore because I just now realized he has facial hair on his chin and upper lip.

"Umm, I'm…I'm 6'2"," he smiles, moving his head forward.

With his help, I fall off him and sit on the bed. And by "with his help," I mean that he just pushed me off. I involuntarily took that fall.

I then look at him and size him up as he sits down next to me.

"When I sit on your shoulders I'm not at my full height because I'm not using my legs. So, I would be about 3 feet sitting on your shoulders. So combined…we are about 9'2" put together. My full height is 5'7" so…"

"So, you would have to stand on my shoulders and jump the other three feet," he interrupts, finishing my thought.

I sigh, thinking *Yeah* in a sad way. But I let out a small smile to cover the fear.

My eyes wander back up at the painting as I feel him looking at me.

"You don't trust me?" he asks, touching my shoulder.

His touch was random, causing me to jump. Standing up quickly, I lean against the wall to play it off while staring at him.

"I am sorry, I didn't mean to scare you!"

"No, it's not your fault. I tend to jump at unpredictable physical touch, even if it's platonic."

I look back up at the ceiling, avoiding eye contact.

"That seems like a sensitive topic, so I won't pry into that. But you can trust me. I won't let you fall, and besides, jumping is the only plan we have. We can't grab a broom because that's in the kitchen and we probably won't survive long enough to bring it back. Also, the bed's too far away from the painting and won't give you the needed height even if we had you jump off of that," he explains, flushing out his thoughts.

Yes, Mr. Obvious, I know, I respond in my head.

All of a sudden, I feel Richard's arms wrap around my legs as he lifts me. I place my hands on his shoulders and stare into his eyes.

Mostly for balance, don't think of anything weird. Just a force of habit…yeah.

My face turns red, quick, as he stares into me, not through me but so far into me it's as if he's no stranger to the path to my soul.

He then places me on the bed - I'm standing up now - and turns around. I jump onto his back and firmly grab his shoulders as I climb up with my legs. A slight panic fills my soul, but I try to brush it off. He is moving a lot as I crouch on his shoulders.

He finds his balance.

My heart beats fast, nearly skipping beats. I wrap my arms over his neck.

"Just stand up, you are almost there."

"I can't."

Memories flood my head as I sit there crouching on his shoulders. *Please don't get triggered. Please don't get triggered. Xena, you're fine,* my thoughts reassure me.

Knowing that I just want to get off.

In a quick motion, Richard grabs my legs tightly. I feel my body being thrown in the air, and I hit the painting off the roof with my hand.

I wasn't flailing my arms or anything, my hand just hit it because it grazed the roof.

The painting falls to the ground as Richard moves out of the way, dodging it. Closing my eyes as I fall back down. His arm wraps under my knees and my back, right before my body touches the ground. A small scream came out while covering my mouth. Opening my eyes, he gently puts me on the ground. On my feet I push him hard. His back hits the bed.

I back away from him. My back hits the wall causing me to jump.

"Fuck you, what was that? No heads up or warning! You just tossed me up in the air!" I snap.

My voice rings loud in the room as Mark peaks around the corner, looking at us. Then goes back out of view.

Forgot he was there.

"I'm sorry, but you weren't going to jump on your own free will. At least I caught you. So, you're safe."

He raises his voice as I roll my eyes, looking at the painting. I can feel his slight anger.

The frame is broken, and a note is sticking out the sides. Even on the verge of tears, I grab the note.

Memories of being tossed in the air and getting hurt and bruised replay in my head. *"You're safe, it's just blood." "I know you want it." "You can always leave…once I'm finished."* Until my traumas are the only thought running through my head. Now in full motion pictures. *"XENA, COME BACK!!"*

Slowly feeling a panic settling into my soul again. My eyes take a quick glance at Richard.

He leans close to me.

It's too hard to concentrate on the note, and Richard could probably tell that. So, he reaches for it. I drop the note instantly. Fighting the tears trying to fall out of my eyes. I slide down the wall, covering my ears with my shaking hand.

Burying them in my knees, while looking away from him at the wall.

"I-I'm sorry for yelling, please don't hurt me," I say in a muffled tone rocking back and forth.

"~~It's not your fault~~ *You're to blame, now come here*," he says.

Tears run down my face as he grabs the note and sits down in front of me.

A little bit of space between us.

"~~Xena~~ *XENA…* ~~are you okay~~ *kneel down* ~~say something~~ *I WILL BREAK YOU. You have no one to run to.*"

I start crying harder, rocking. Repeating Richard's name over and over again between tears. *He feels so far, he'll never be here, I don't want him to see me like this… I-*

"Baby, it's just me, Richard, it's just you and me again," he soothes. "What do you need me to do?"

I can't begin to speak. I sit there trying to stop crying as he reassures me that everything is fine.

My brain races a mile a minute as my emotions feel uncontrollable. Constant thoughts of the physical abuse my ex did spin around in my head as I pull my legs tighter against my chest.

I'm hyperventilating.

My body feels numb.

But even with that, I just keep my eyes closed and try to focus on the fact that it's just Richard. No other man but him.

My body feels weak.

My head is throbbing.

"Xena, breathe. Deep breath in…deep breath out," he says, doing the breathing. "Look at me…deep breath in…deep breath out," he says, tilting my chin up to him with one finger.

I can't make eye contact, so I look at his chest through tears. We breathe together like that for a few more seconds. I just want him to hold me. But he would have no way of knowing that because the words feel trapped inside of me. Chained to a rock sinking in a river.

I stare at the carpet, tears hitting loudly as the sounds around me start to fade out.

"Thank you, love. I'm sorry I freaked out on you."

"It's my fault I pushed your boundaries. You were slowly showing me that you couldn't and I wasn't listening," he soothes, holding out his arms.

"I'm sorry!"

My bottom lip shaking, I climb into his arms.

Our chests are touching as I sit on his lap with my arms wrapped over his shoulder. My head nestled in his neck as tears fall harder than before. But the gentle motion of him rubbing my back makes me feel safer.

He holds me like that for five minutes until the tears stop falling on his shoulder.

"Are you ready to continue?" he asks under his breath.

"Concerned to stay stationary too long with everything going around us?" I slightly laugh, making him let out a small smile.

"No. I've been through this fear before. The sun just set, and the note says we must go to the swimming center. I want to know so I can prevent myself from triggering you again," he soothes, holding me.

I squeeze him hard for a moment before loosening up.

Making a long pause as I sniffle, resting my chin on his shoulder.

"My last relationship was physically abusive, he use to throw me around and bruise me as well as my father was too til the days he passed. I'm fine now."

I sniffle, wiping my face.

Richard then slides off his scarf, wiping off my tears with it.

"I'm sorry you had to go through that. I didn't know."

"I know you didn't know. And I had so many opportunities to tell you, but that would put everyone as risk if I did. Besides, you would have looked at me differently when I met you and your dad," I laugh nervously, but talking faster, breathing in sharply.

"I didn't say "I didn't know" for it to come off as you should have told me. I said that because you're strong and hold so much inside you that I can tell that you forget that people don't know. I don't see you any different than I did twenty seconds ago before you told me. Abuse doesn't define you love, it's my responsibility to give you the boundaries you deserve."

I faintly smile as a few more tears fall out of my eyes. Richard then smiles back and leans in close to me. Kissing me on the forehead.

Then sets his chin on top of my head, sighing deeply.

"Does your ex live around here?"

"No, and before you start, he's leaving me alone now. He got a new girlfriend, and Lowell threatened him and broke his arm. She didn't know anything he was just being a bother to her."

"Well, I'll always be here, okay?" he adds. "Let me take some of the burden off."

I don't even know if he could protect me or if he'd even stay when in trouble, we've never been in a situation outside of this one for me really have ever needed to assess if he really would keep the door open for me.

But it's the thought that counts so I smile in my thoughts, nodding my head.

"Thank you, Richard."

"For what?"

"Being patient- holding and speaking to me softly with good intentions."

"One day you'll learn how I wouldn't be here if not for you," he says, wiping away some of my tears slowly.

"I love you."

Our eyes connect deeply for a few seconds, and he breaks eye contact. He's never said he loved me before.

"I love you more."

I then stick my tongue at him, as he helps me off the floor. I dry the rest of my tears while he sticks the note in his pocket. We walk over to the door, but before we get through it, I touch his shoulder. Causing him to look behind him, at me.

"Promise me that If I ever die in this game, you will leave me!" I faintly smile.

He looks at me with broken eyes, raising an eyebrow, as I glance away into the hallway. I'm scared to die, yes, but I also don't see myself living long anyway. Regardless of the game, I always feel like I'm about to die, so this is just a bonus situation to my fear.

"You're random Xena, I'm not promising that. Besides, you hate promises, remember?" he responds, with his hand on my shoulder.

I pat it.

"Yes, I do. But I think you can keep this one." *Because we both know you wouldn't bare to stay.*

I say, putting a finger on his chest so we can make the promise. He then rolls his eyes and puts his fingers on mine.

"Yeah," he frowns, glancing away. "Right."

We both draw an X on each other's chest with our fingers and bump fists.

Mark is gone, yet the door is open. If he was going to leave, he should have just closed it.

I put Richard's backpack on his back and grab our phones. We both slowly poke our heads out of the door and creep down to the lounge.

Silence, of course, fills the room as blood lays everywhere. When Richard and I see that the coast is clear, we make a run for the door. He places his hand on the doorknob and opens it, letting me go out first.

"Wait," Mark yells behind us.

I turn around, as he walks towards us from the kitchen. But just before he gets past the kitchen, the lights cut off.

Knowing that's not a good sign, Richard and I quickly walk out of the door and crack it open. I peek inside to see if Mark is coming but all I see is a blue light hovering over him. Once he looked at the light, it exploded in his face. The last sound he made was a blood-curdling scream.

The lights cut back on and all I see is him lying on the ground with knives in his body. He's gurgling blood that is settling in his mouth from his throat.

On the verge of throwing up, I quickly close the door and turn around looking at Richard.

I give him the look of "He didn't make it" and we walk down the hallway.

Fast pace.

Richard leads the way as we run down three flights of stairs to get to the main floor. We walk towards the west wing since the swimming pool center is in an individual building next to the west wing.

As we pass the split staircase leading to the lawn, I see something in the trees.

Pulling on Richard so he could stop walking. I grab the flashlight out of his bag. Shining it at the trees.

It's Lowell and Christopher climbing down a tree, while wolves are lying on the ground by them. I didn't even know we had wolves in this town; they're so beautiful.

I waved them over to us and they sprinted towards us. Just as they are running up the stairs, one wolf gets up and looks at all of us. Gazing into our souls. We all pause for a second, creeping down the hallway in hopes that they don't see us moving. But to no one's surprise, it trips over its friend before sprinting towards us. Causing the rest to follow as the four of us run towards the swim center. They're nearly feet away from us but all you must do is be quicker than the person behind you to survive

Which is hard because all four of us are so fast that none of us are actually far in front or behind each other.

That adrenaline kicked in and we all turned into track stars. Never did I glance backward.

I just focus on the soft grass, the dark sky, and the light of the swim center getting closer and closer to us.

When we make it to the double door entrance, we quickly swing it open, run through, and close it behind us. Just as it closes, we hear the wolves on the other side of the door howling and scratching at the door. Christopher lets out a huge sigh of relief as Lowell barricades the door with the nearest conveniently placed chairs.

Richard and I just back up from the door and look around the swim center. The pool is huge and the clear water makes the turquoise tiles look vibrant. Freshwater lays on the side of the pool as if someone has already been in here.

As I walk from one side of the pool to the other, it is hard not to notice that the storage closet door is open.

I don't want to investigate alone.

Waving at the other three, the only one who is looking at me is Lowell. She cocks her head to the side and runs over towards me. I slowly walk into the storage closet. Once we make it inside, the door quickly closes behind us. The sound of the door locking can be heard.

This was a trap; I think to myself as we run over to the door. It won't open. But we try anyway.

Just as we start beating on it to get the other's attention, the light inside turns blue. Making it easier to see the room.

There is sports equipment everywhere and hockey sticks in the corners. This room feels terrifying, so Lowell and I remain standing by the door and keep knocking on it so the boys can let us out. Or know that we are in here.

When they finally come to the door, they jiggle the doorknob, but it still doesn't open. Richard says "Ouch!" from the other side, so I touch the doorknob again. It is burning.

"Don't panic, we will get you out," Christopher announces from the other side.

"Wait! We need them to stay in there," Richard whispers to Christopher, loud enough for us to hear.

"Did you say stay? Why?" Lowell yells.

"The note Xena and I found earlier say that the clue is in the closet."

"Can you slide it under the door so we can read it?" I ask as Richard slides it under the door.

"Already ahead of you," Richard exclaims. *I bet he smiled all dorky when he said that.*

Grabbing it, Lowell and I read it in our heads.

It says:

Locked in the closet you will need to be
Near the pool to set me free
For a simulation of your true feelings
But do not double-cross me

Just ask her as you please
Which could make your birthday better
Or be the best opportunity to clear the air

"Guys I understand this one," Lowell exclaims.

"Congratulations Lowell, you finally understand one of the riddles," Christopher sarcastically replies.

I giggle but clear my throat and look down once Lowell glances at me. My heart is beating out of my chest as the darkness in this room sends chills down my spine. I'm scared of the dark. I keep my mind focused on how *Richard is the only one who understands that which is why I feel so safe... at least I'm wearing his brown shirt.*

"Finally understanding. Very funny," she mocks, turning around.

She starts walking around the closet and moving things around.

I feel like the note is making us look for a jump rope because "*double-cross*" reminds me of jumping roping or double dutch. I walk over to the weights and workout equipment to see if there are ropes as Lowell stands near the ball rack. This storage closet is the biggest one on campus; the majority of the sports equipment is here.

"S-so what did you take from this riddle?" I ask, grabbing a green jump rope.

"Well, I only understand the first two lines, but I don't know what to look for. I just know what to do with what we find."

"Okay," I say, trying to relax my breathing, handing her the jump rope. "Tell me what to do."

I then see a note under me as I look back down.

Jump and share but ~~don't stop~~

~~If the ropes collides then something is aimed for the eyes~~

The rest of the words are scratched over making them illegible. Let's just hope that the illegible part isn't bad.

Grabbing another green jump rope for myself, Lowell starts to jump. But the light turns off once I start jumping.

It is pitch black.

The only sound I could hear was the air pressure from Lowell and I swinging the ropes. I feel a slow panicking feeling form in my chest.

I yell in my thoughts *I really need Richard right now!,* knowing that's not going to make him show.

"I can't see you, but I feel like the note wants me to ask you stuff," Lowell whispers.

“Do you have any idea of what you want to ask?”

“Questions that I have always wanted to ask you I guess,” she giggles nervously. "I'll ask three. It's a lucky number."

The single light in the ceiling then turns blue. I let out a sigh of relief as we face each other. Jumping rope. The blue light above shines on us like a spotlight on stage.

Everything else in the room is still dark.

“Umm...so, were you born in this town?” she asks, breathing in deeply.

“No. My mom and I moved here for work when I was 14.”

"Oh, well at least you don't have to worry about having a golden birthday."

She pauses. Probably thinking that there is a possibility of me still having one. "What do you like to do for fun?"

"Other than art, I guess it would be exploring the town," I reply, trying to control my breathing.

I’m already tired due to sprinting from the wolves earlier. Along with the feeling of me about to break down.

"That's cool. Our town is huge so maybe I can go with you sometime. Show you my favorite parts," she smiles. "Though, I mostly travel on my skates."

"Same," I giggle, saying “I have skates too” in a happy tone.

Taking in a loud breath.

She then smiles at me as the light turns green.

It then goes back to blue.

Lowell looks like she is thinking about how to phrase her last question as I laugh at the silly faces she makes when she thinks. I feel my body start jumping closer to Lowell, but I keep my distance, so our ropes don’t hit each other.

"I know that we are both tired of jumping rope so I will ask an easy question. Why couldn't we have a decent conversation after your training day?" she asks, raising an eyebrow.

I wasn’t expecting that.

As I think of my answer my jump rope accidentally crashed into hers. Jumping, startled, I let it go while it gets tangled with hers. I then laugh at my clumsiness and look into her unbothered eyes. Leaving it on the ground.

"Well, people…it's probably because…yeah no, people are constantly trying to get your attention at work. Also, our class schedule is different, and that guy wouldn't leave me alone. Maybe I was just…nervous...because it feels like I have to compete for your attention."

She laughs at my reply and makes a confused face. I just roll my eyes at her while grabbing the jump ropes and throwing them to the side.

The light doesn't go back to normal, but I still go over to open the door. It's still locked.

I answered the question, though. What is this creature wanting me to admit? That I may like her or something?

I turn back around, slowly, looking at her.

The blue light starts to light up brighter. Blinking every 3 seconds. Revealing the dark parts of the room for 1 second.

In the corner of my eye, I see a slit in the wall. It's a triangle hole. Starting at it, I feel the room drop fast in temperature. Something's coming out of the hole. Lowell is positioned directly in the shooting range.

An arrow with a blue light on the tip flies from the wall. In quick motions, I reach out and grab the front of her pants. The arrow flies where her head was before I moved her. Pulling her closer to me while my eyes follow the light. My back hits the door as she braces herself to prevent a collision between us two.

Her hand is next to my head. I can feel her light breathing on my neck.

"Y-you were going to die." I swallow nervously, staring at the ceiling.

Letting her go.

The arrow is stuck in the wall to the right of me.

"Thanks," she pauses, slightly laughing from fear. "But I-I just don't understand how you are competing for my attention. You didn't answer the question truthfully or fully. Other than that, the light would have turned green."

Taking a deep breath, I grab her hand and pull it down off the door. I hear another arrow shoot from the wall, but I don't know where.

Lowell yells, “Duck!” while pulling my shoulders in, hard, covering me while we are crouching. I look up through her arms. My heart is racing faster.

The arrow lands on the door where my head was before I crouched. There is a red light on this one though.

I slide my legs down so I can sit instead of crouch. She places her soft hand in mine, her breathing as fast as my racing heart.

Her body over mine feels so warm. So safe. So comfortable. Yet she moves her arms off my shoulder and back.

Still keeping close in distance, her hand remains on top of mine.

I roll my eyes, faintly smiling while letting go of her hand.

“I don't know what I'm supposed to say. Am I supposed to say that I can’t hold a decent conversation because every time I talk to you, we either get interrupted or I get lost in your beautiful ivy green eyes?"

The light above flicks green before going pitch black.

"Oh," I look off to my right, embarrassed.

My eyes are closed because it's more comfortable.

Great, I guess that was the answer then. I really thought I said that in my head, I think to myself in annoyance.

I can't see her anymore. All I know is that she is a few ways in front of me.

The only thing heard is the sound of my breathing and loud heartbeat. Doubt she can hear it though. “So, you get lost in my eyes?” Lowell adds in a soft voice, amused.

“Shut up,” I joke, playfully rolling my eyes.

Something then collides loudly with the floor in the far corner of the room. Causing me to jump.

I don't make a noise.

A raspy, intercom-type voice then starts speaking:

Mm you answered the questions to your best ability
Now it's up to you to find a way out.
I promise you it's harder than it looks

It lets out an evil laugh then the intercom cuts off.

I didn't even know there was one here. It's an odd spot. Maybe it's not even in here but connected through where Richard is at. That would make more sense.

"Are you guys okay?" Christopher yells. "We heard the intercom come on."

"Yes, it's just pitch black and getting colder by the second," Lowell replies.

"We are trying to get you out. Xena, are you doing fine?" Richard asks.

"Yeah," I say standing up.

I can hear the lock start rustling. He must be trying to break it or pry it off.

Feeling the walls around us with my left hand, Lowell grabs my right hand. I jump at first, but she says, "it's just me" and uses me to help pull herself up. Her knee lets out a popping sound.

"I'm going to feel around. Come with me?" I whisper, not knowing where she is.

"Do I have a choice?"

"Always," I say walking forwards. "I would never force you to do something you didn't want to."

"Really?" She says surprised, then clears her throat. "I mean, of course, I have a choice. I'll come."

She walks behind me as I feel on the walls down to the floor. Like I did in the open mic room with Richard. Lowell places one of her hands on my lower back. Temperature is dropping rapidly.

She taps nervously on it to keep her calm. Using the other hand to help vocally tell me what's surrounding us.

That's when we both step on ropes under us. We must be where the jump ropes are at. On the opposite side of the room.

Continuing to rub my hand on the wall, Lowell stops walking. Gripping my waist softly, so I stop walking.

"Are you okay?"

No response.

"Lowell?"

She stops tapping or touching me at all. Scared, I reach out but I can't feel her. *She was close earlier, why can't I feel her now?* I think.

"Lowell?" I whisper.

"Yes," she sighs deeply.

"Why the hell are you not responding? Where are you?" I say with concern, slightly irritated because she scared me.

"Oops, I zoned out and got lightheaded. I didn't mean to scare you. I'm sitting on the floor now, see."

She reaches her hand up, feeling for me. She then touches my legs, hitting them, saying "It's me" as she tries to pull me down. Once on the floor in front of her, she pulls herself into my lap and wraps her arms and feet around my back saying, "Better."

I can tell that she's smiling. Especially as she lays her head down on my chest.

She then relaxes completely.

She's exhausted, I know. The cold isn't helping either.

I lay my head on hers. My lips casually place themselves softly on her head. Then I let go and breathe deeply, covering my red face by laying my head on hers. My heart beats aggressively, as her arms are still wrapped around my waist.

Damn my heart and mentality, I think to myself. Lowell's face is feeling hot to the touch now, but her head is still lying on my shoulder.

"Are you okay? I'm sorry for that, Lowell. I didn't ask."

"N-no, I-mm…I'm fine. You're good, Xena."

I know it was unintentional, but I loved the way she exhaustingly moaned my name.

Comfortable with each other and staying warm is the only form of heat we have left. We sit like that in the dark for what feels like 15-30 minutes. I don't want to think that we are dying but we might be. Goosebumps and exhaustion waving over me. I try to fight it but I don't know how long I can hold it. Part of me thinks Lowell already gave in because her body relaxes more. Almost in a floppy manner and she stops talking to me.

"Are you still there Lowell?" I say, rubbing the back of her head. Behind her hair, it feels cut. She must have an undercut.

I try not to panic and think of the worst, as I rub her back and face. She's heating up extremely.

I think she passed out. I once knew a girl who did the same thing but I forgot why. I don't know if it was because of the temperature changing or her getting overly scared.

All of a sudden the light turns on fully and the door clicks, indicating that it is finally unlocked. The light from outside shines in the room but behind us. The boys still can't quite see us since we are on the opposite side of the light.

I then shake Lowell but she doesn't move. We need to get out fast before this creature changes its mind.

Deciding to pick her up, I clasp my hands together under her butt. Lifting her and moving her head on my shoulder so I could see. Walking out as quickly as possible. She is a little heavy and curvy for sure, along with being taller than me. Because I work out often, she only feels forty pounds bigger than me.

Trying to escape quickly, I wince as the light pours over my face. Christopher and Richard jump, startled. But Christopher comes over and takes Lowell off of me. Laying her on the floor next to me as I sit down, she is starting to move now. I place my hand on her warm face.

Her eyes start opening.

We all sit there in silence for a moment as she slowly comes back. Her body is weak and she struggles to fully sit up for the next 3 minutes.

"What happened?" She asks softly.

"You passed out," I say, moving my hand.

Richard closes the door.

There's a note in Christopher's hand.

Deep Dive {Lowell}

I'm happy that Xena was already holding me. The last time I passed out randomly, I fell down two flights of wooden stairs.

My emotions almost get the best of me every time I'm near her.

"Wow," I say, clearing my throat.

Christopher helps me up.

My voice echoes through the room, causing Xena and Richard to stare at me, confused.

"I meant wow because we were in the closet for a long time. This has to be the first time being in the closet felt great," I nervously add.

The boys look at me, smiling.

Xena covers her mouth, but she's silently laughing hard under her hand. Her shoulders are bobbing up and down.

"Because we didn't die, of course, ya know."

This is so embarrassing; the walls really didn't have to expose me like that by echoing my voice. *But nice save, Lowell,* I think to myself.

Though I kind of wonder if Xena is interested in the same way I am or if she is just playing with me. 'Cause I'm tired of being led on by straight girls.

But for now, I guess I'll just let it slide. We are playing a life-or-death game so I'm happy that I at least have something to take my mind off of this whole situation.

Smiling, I nudge her as she stands next to me. She nudges me back harder. Then, we start throwing punches but purposely miss each other for fun as we get closer to the pool. I almost push her in.

"Stop bantering, we need to do the next riddle," Christopher announces.

"We still have until sunrise to finish this game and we need to start taking our situation more seriously," Richard adds.

Xena pulls out her phone and shows me what the time is. It's already

11:00 and we have almost 6 hours left until sunrise.

We were going so fast in the beginning. Where did the time go?

"Richard discovered that the next card is at the bottom of the pool, so we need Lowell to dive for it," Christopher announces.

"I haven't swum in five years. How deep is the pool?"

"Well, it did move down while you were in the closet. So…probably 14 feet."

I gulp nervously. Sweating bullets. I've drowned diving 10 feet before without anyone around.

"You want me to add an extra 4 feet to my drowning record," I reply sarcastically. "Sounds great. Why don't we also just go ahead and say our last words to each other now? Don't waste time saying that for later."

"Lowell, listen. All of us are going to be standing by watching to make sure you don't drown. You still hold the record for the deepest diver in town even though you haven't been in the water since your incident. The rest of us can barely swim compared to you, so you have to do it."

"But what if I drown and none of you can get to me? Then how will we survive this game?"

"We won't," Richard shrugs.

"Don't say that." Xena gently punches Richard. "I will swim with you, and we can have a rope tied to our feet. That way you won't be alone, and they can pull us back up if we die."

I think about it for a moment. It is best if we stick together even if we go in the water. But it's all too much.

"I don't know, guys," I sigh.

"I know you're scared, but you can do this. All you have to do is put your trust in us and I promise we will get you out of this alive. Your swimming instincts will kick back because swimming is not just a sport for you. It relaxes you and makes you feel at home, so it triumphs over your fears. You'll make it! I dote you too much to lose you over a recreation," Christopher consoles.

"Thank you...I think."

Richard then whispers to him, "Tone it down. No need to get all motivational speaker on us."

"That was too much?" Christopher whispers back.

"A little bit, yes," Xena whispers to him.

He then laughs as I feel a rope being tied around my ankle. Richard had triple knotted it so it wouldn't come loose. He goes to do the same to Xena. Faintly smiling at her and hugging before walking away. Both of the boys head over to the side of the pool. *He works fast,* I think to myself.

Xena and I follow.

Taking my shoes off, I can feel the cold, wet floor. Feels weird yet safe. The pool is clear, making it easy to see the note on the bottom. As Xena and I stand at the end of the deepest side, the boys cover their eyes.

It confuses me until I glance at Xena. She is taking her shirt off.

Her small body frame looks perfect as the ceiling lights make her skin glow so beautifully. But I quickly dart my eyes from her. Covering my face too. I know that she knows that I was staring for a split second because she throws her shirt at me.

Don't look, don't look. The floor... Yes, the floor is sooo nice. Is that tile? I think to myself while staring at the floor nervously.

Xena then randomly starts laughing as I take my shirt off and toss it at her. It quickly goes silent. She slides my shirt from over one eye, peaking at me. I can see a slight amount of blood on the top part of my pants. I wonder whose it is.

Xena then pushes me into the pool for no reason.

I shiver while the cold water climbs up my back. I float on the surface to pull myself out of the pool and dangle my feet in the water. Yet Xena sits right in front of me. Stopping me from getting out of the pool. She leans forward. It must be something in the water because my heart feels different towards her. More tension. A good difference but scary nonetheless.

The boys look back at us as they continue to stand on the side. Talking amongst each other like teachers do when the principal walks in to hold a conversation.

"Are you ready?" she asks, scrunching her nose and looking up at the boys. They dart their vision away from us.

"Yeah. Are you okay?"

"Yeah, no I'm good. I just want you to make it out of this alive."

"Why wouldn't I? I have you to save me, remember?" I smile, splashing water at her.

She smiles, then helps me out of the water. Coldness falls over me as we both stand up, looking into the water nervously. I squeeze Xena's hand. Then shake off my nerves.

She dives first.

A huge splash sound comes from the water as I jump in after her.

It gets warmer as I swim towards the bottom, holding my breath. Not warmer in a "someone peed in the pool" type of way, but in a "turning the shower water too hot" way. On top of that, I see different shades of blue pass my eyes. The note looks like it is so far away.

The rope on my ankle gets tighter as flashbacks of my drowning start to come to me.

As I start to slow down, I glance at Xena swimming next to me. It is only out of pure fear that I grab her hand. She seemed to not care, especially since I let go after a few seconds. She is standing still now. Looking at something in the far distance.

On the other side of the pool.

I continue diving.

Counting how many seconds I am holding my breath is the only thing I could do to get it off my mind. Felt like something was choking me but internally. The water pressure tightens on my body.

Panic hits me at this point. I try to hold it together. The water feels so warm and relaxing right now. Like I could breathe it in. Sleep.

40…41…42…I grab the note and bounce off the bottom of the pool. Only going up six feet as I slowly try to swim up, the rope feels looser on my ankle. That's when I look at Xena.

She is now also swimming up along with me.

Nearly inches from the surface, something starts pulling her back down to the bottom. I grab her hand tightly to stop her from going past me. A dark shadow fills the opposite side of the pool.

Closest to Xena.

She screams quietly.

Air bubbles from her mouth float to the top of the pool. Blood rising around us too. I can hear the boy frantically talking above the water.

As she gets pulled farther into the dark, her body halfway through it, she looks at me. I can feel myself starting to cry. She's terrified.

Red blood fills around her face before she fully goes in. Air bubbles float up as I scream for her.

Her hand slips out of my grasp.

I never saw her again after that.

Next thing I knew, the darkness spread over me. Leaving it pitch black.

Scared, I tried to keep swimming up. Struggling against the water. It felt like thick mud.

Oxygen becoming a deep necessity.

I see someone's hand reaching in the water. Grabbing it as they pull me up, I cough up water on the floor. Their hand, feeling spiky, hits my back to better help me. Our bodies are inches away.

That's when I look up at them. They look dark, and spiky all over. I didn't get a great look because the next thing I knew, I was being pushed back into the water.

Their hands now holding me down. Water over my face. Eyes rolling back as I take a breath.

My body jerked for the last time.

Through The Curtains {Lowell's Mark}

Lowell slowly opens her eyes, fixing them at the ceiling. Unable to move. Feeling lifeless.

Red curtains swing around her head. I watch her mysteriously through the curtain knowing that she can't see me. Knowing that her back is sore. Smiling, I touch my empty chest and stare at her human features. A perfect set of lungs, I ponder knowing that mine is missing. Scared at her quick motion, my back hits the wall as she grabs the curtain with her right hand. Using it to help her sit up.

Creeping close to her, I hover behind. She's perfect for me. Thanks for finally getting it right, love!

I feel a strong presence from behind me. Turning around I see nothing. I shake it off, lifting my hands to stretch, and pull myself to my feet. A piece of the rope is on my ankle. Looked like it had been ripped apart.

Am I alone? *Are you?*

Feeling the presence again, I turn back around. Nothing's there.

My heart races faster as I keep staring into the darkness. I start to see a figure. Swaying.

"*I know you,*" a soft voice says from the darkness.

Not being able to see, I quickly back up. Facing the direction the voice came, while my heart races faster.

"*Please, don't be scared. We are similar, you and I, in more ways than one,*" they add. "*You can respond.*"

I swallow hard.

My voice trembles as I say, "What do you want me to say?"

"*Nothing too special, love,*" she pauses.

Walking into the light.

"*Are you scared?*"

She has hip dips and thin, light blue, translucent hair. Looks like something straight out of a ghost movie. Her eyes are cold like ice as she towers over me. 12 feet tall from what I can see. Not to mention her skin radiates a beautiful lavender aura. A beauty to the eyes, like a goddess.

She speaks softly, almost bringing comfort to me.

"N-not anymore."

"*Good,*" she smiles softly.

Creeping over to me.

"*This should be quick then.*"

Her smile slowly turns into an evil one as her hands grab mine. She spins me around, pinning my arm behind my back. She scratches it painfully with her nails. It throbs in pain as I remain quiet. Blood trickles down slowly. She licks it, swirling her tongue around her finger while her eyes stare deep into my soul.

Her right hand tilts my head back as she floats over me.

My cheeks turn red.

She then places her pointer finger on my chest. My skin feels like it's being burned by the touch. I bite my lip hard.

"*Since I've been waiting for this moment, I'll give you a choice,*" she says in a deep voice.

One that sounds rather masculine. Nothing like her voice from before, but still nice.

"*You can either stay here with me and be given all your deepest desires,*" she grins, pointing around the room.

I can't see how a room full of red curtains would be anyone's desire, so I shake my head no. Maybe she was supposed to show me something.

"*Or you can go back into the game.*"

"I choose the game," I respond loudly, wincing in pain.

She takes her finger off of me and lets me go. Stepping back.

"*As you wish,*" she smiles. "*But if you're anything like me, you'll come back. I know you will.*"

She then puts her hand under her mouth. Blowing green mist down at me.

"Who are you?" I ask, rubbing my eyes. The smoke is messing with my eyesight.

"*The only spirit here that can help you.*"

Don’t Test Me {Lowell}

I jolt up gasping for air. Coughing up a large amount of water.

Looking around to see where I’m at, Christopher is in tears and Richard chucks my shirt at me so I can wipe off my face.

It hit me harder than expected.

Confused, I see that Xena is next to me.

Her body lays on the cold floor with multiple cuts on it as her pulse is faded. Hands covered the most in blood like she was fighting something. But her feet look like she was walking on broken glass.

I assume that the place I was in earlier was just a nightmare. Or maybe most of it was and whoever hurt her must have cut her.

"Don't do this Xena. Come on, come back!" Christopher cries.

Those words make both Richard and I keep our silence.

Christopher checks her pulse multiple times before shaking his head no.

Richard looks away from us with a blank expression. Even her lifeless body feels more alive than Richards eyes currently.

It took a minute, but it just now dawns on me that she is dead. Tears start falling down my face as I punch the wall. It's my fault. I let her hand go. My anger and sadness are uncontrollable, and I want nothing more than to trade spots with her. *It was my fault for choosing to come back to the game,* I think to myself. *Maybe it was the wrong choice.*

“She’s dead.”

"Lowell, don't announce that," Christopher whispers, on the verge of tears.

"She is, though. CPR didn't work," Richard replies.

"No, she is not. She will come back."

"Christopher, she is not coming back," I say in a flat tone.

"She will. I just know she… "

"She’s dead," Richard interrupts, sighing. "Let her go!"

I glance at Richard, as we both stare at Christopher, staring at Xena.

Christopher is still holding her as I stop punching the wall and stand next to Richard. I am confused as to why Richard isn't crying because for me, it feels like my heart is being ripped out. In more ways than one.

I try not to blame myself for her cuts. Or for letting go of her hand. She should have never dived with me.

"You two should go," Christopher announces after moments of silence.

"No!" I rebuke, softly.

"Leave! We can't waste time because the game is not going to stop. As long as you finish the game then we can all live."

"By all, you mean us three?"

"No, possibly everyone who played. It's an uncertain outcome but sometimes things go back to normal and sometimes the dead stay dead." Richard explains.

"Why didn't you mention that in the beginning?" I roll my eyes at him.

Then hand him the note because I can't see it through my tears. He reads it aloud, telling us our next location is at the library.

My chest throbs in pain but I try to ignore it.

As we get ready to go, Christopher sits against the wall, still holding Xena's lifeless body. His eyes puffy.

"I will meet you in thirty minutes. If she comes back around then I want to make sure she is not alone," he faintly smiles.

"The two of us have experienced our birthdays differently with the way they ended, so we don't know what will happen when the sun rises. We might as well just…" Richard pauses, glancing at the door. Then lets out a painful sigh. "We might as well just leave her."

"That is a funny suggestion coming from you. No thank you. All my friends survived at the end of my golden birthday because I did not leave them alone. Every time we left an injured person alone today, they died."

I mumble "She is already dead though" as they ignore me.

"At least you had a positive outcome. None of mine came back to life at sunrise. I had to move high schools so people would stop calling me a murderer," Richard snaps. "All but Xena called me one. Even then, I still messed us up."

Christopher tries to adjust her head positioning to be more comfortable and Richard bites his lip. For a moment reaches out at her body and then pulls back.

"Can you please be soft! She doesn't like to be handled so dangerously."

He heads towards the door after he makes that statement. As this is already too much to handle, I think he's just in shock right now. I wonder why he's not fighting to be the one to stay.

"I'm sorry," Christopher mumbles.

The pain in Richard's voice is hard to not pick up, but over these two weeks, I've learned that he struggles to show his pain.

"Lowell, take care of him, please!"

"I will as long as you take care of Xena for us. Stay optimistic," I smile, hugging him. Whispering, "and be gentle with her body- that's all he has now if she doesn't come back."

Christopher knods.

For a split second, I thought I saw her chest rise and fall slightly, but it was nothing.

Running over to Richard, he slowly creaks open the door. We both look out to see if the wolves are still here, but luckily the coast is clear. Sprinting towards the main college building, we don't look back once as we go up a flight of stairs. The library was on the second floor closer to the east wing but we came up the stairs in the west wing.

It is quiet and half of the second floor is dark.

The light flickers above us as we walk in silence. Richard and I are not that close and people say we have grown a weird, aggressive friendship. Though it's better than the way I act towards Zoe, because I actually kinda like Richard.

Oh shoot, Zoe, I think to myself. I forgot about her.

"We have to go back downstairs to the first floor," I announce to Richard.

"Why?"

"Christopher and I told Zoe we would come back for her, so she is still in the clinic."

"Did she get hurt and you two decided to leave her so she wouldn't slow you down?"

"Yes."

I am shocked by his guessing skills, which remind me of a less scary version of Xena's skills.

Anyway, we turn around and quickly make our way back down the stairs. The faster we move through the dark desolate hallway, the longer we survive. The first-floor hallway is the same as earlier with Christopher, along with the lawn still being empty. Richard follows behind me as I lead us to the clinic. When we arrive, I open the door and close it behind us.

The room is the same as before and Deondra is still dead on one of the beds. Though Zoe is laying down, with her phone shining bright on her face. Richard looks unfazed by the fact that Deondra is dead, but I don't blame him. Neither of us got to know her since she was closer to Emil, Mark, and Zoe. On top of that, we have all seen so many people die that at this rate we are sitting in this traumatizing experience together. All I know for sure is that if anyone comes back from the dead, we won't be fazed by it.

Richard then flicks the light on so they can see better. Lowell creeps over to Zoe. Richard checks his phone, letting out a sigh of relief, smiling, as Lowell raises her eyebrow. He must have gotten good news. Zoe is laying down on the bed, snoring her head off. As Lowell slowly opens Zoe's eyes, blood gushes out of them. I laugh.

Lowell's eyes go wide as she swallows my vomit, covering her mouth with her hand. Yet she still decides to take a better look at her bloody face.

"What might you be spying on?" Z asks, coming up behind me. "Why are you mumbling to yourself all creepy-like?"

"I'm just observing, Zilla," I say, glancing at her. "Narrating, if you must say."

'Disinteresting, I presume? Perhaps you might join me in visiting a few of the pine overcoats to have some real fun," she grins, blowing me a kiss. Motioning me closer with her finger.

Torn between watching the kids and going with her, I sigh and proceed to walk with her. These kids are fine...but Zilla on the other hand... After all this time she's still so alluring, *I reflect in my thoughts, smiling.*

I take a better look at Zoe.

A pool of blood settles in her mouth like spit does when cartoon characters sleep with their mouths open. Her eyes must have opened because of me shaking her. Her pulse is registering but is weak.

No need to wait around since she is going to be dead soon. We have the opportunity to get her back by winning the game. I respect the fact that Zoe didn't leave. Though there's no obvious evidence that points to how she got this way.

Looking at Richard, I shake my head "no" as he reopens the door. He walks out in silence and heads back up the stairs. We walk through the dimly lit second-floor hallway towards the library. Richard is upset, and I wish he would just tell me because this silence is terrible.

"How do you feel?"

Silence.

His lack of answering makes me a little upset but I let it slide.

He starts walking a little faster as I patiently wait for his response. Continuing to try and get him to talk, he doesn't answer any of my questions. Out of impulse, I run up, grab his wrist, and turn him to face me.

"Lowell, just drop it. Can't you tell that I don't want to talk about Xena?" he snaps, pushing me off of him.

"Just answer my questions. Xena died and all you have been being is- well...I don't know how to describe it. It's almost like you don't care about her death."

His whole demeanor and face then drop cold.

"Don't test me, Lowell. I was in her life long before we met you, and the way I mourn is my business."

He turns away from me and walks forward further.

We approach the dark part of the hallway and stand still for a moment. Right before he goes inside, I pull him back, pushing him into the wall again.

"Stop pushing me or else…" he threatens.

"Or else what? You're going to hit me?" I tease, laughing.

He chuckle softly in amusement, rolling his eyes. "Xena would never forgive me if I hurt you," he sighs deeply. "This honestly feels like I'm abandoning her all over again."

He then pushes me off. Glancing away.

Those words claw at my heart, leaving me speechless. His emotions for Xena do cut deep like my emotions for Christopher but what does he mean by "abandoning her again?" Is this about the high school murdering thing he mentioned earlier?

I partially wish I had a close relationship like theirs.

"I am sorry for your loss. It was ignorant for me to say you didn't care."

"It was."

It then goes silent. The only thing heard is the tapping of our feet hitting the ground as we walk.

"How did y'all even meet?" I ask to break the silence.

"I'd rather not say. You'd look at us differently if I told you."

"I won't judge you two."

"Lowell…I promise you will. If not me, you'd judge her for sure."

A sad expression then falls across his face as I realize that him not crying doesn't make him any less hurt than the rest of us. To my surprise, I can't be the only one who feels like this game has made us closer. Making me forget that our individual best friend duos just combined days ago. Though I can understand that Richard just doesn't want to cry like this is the end for her.

He's not ready to accept it.

As we approach the last lit light hanging from the ceiling, darkness is in front of us. We can't turn back since the library is the dark part of the hallway inches away. The atmosphere is cold as I look at Richard motioning him forwards, walking through.

Not scared by the fact that I can't see anything, I walk along the wall. Richard follows behind me, keeping close. There is a sign glowing that reads "Library," so I open the door under the sign. Just before I walk in, I feel a gigantic amount of body heat behind me.

Turning around to see what it is, a red light positions itself with a little space between us. It reminds me of the blue dot that I keep seeing, but nothing happens. I try to go through the library door but every time I move the red dot gets closer. All of a sudden, the light goes over my arm and it gets dark. Meaning I can't see anymore.

Fear fills me so I run into the library, closing the door behind Richard and me. We then hear laughing. Loud, creepy laughing echoes through the room.

The last thing I felt was my body land in Richard's arms.

Just Kiss Already {Xena's Mark}

I pull myself up against the wall and notice that everyone is gone. Just a few seconds ago, I was in the water with Lowell. Where is she? Darkness spread over us, and someone had grabbed my mouth. Holding me down. Scary, nonetheless. And I almost got away because I bit their hand, causing them to bleed. But they scratched me. The last thing I saw was red fill around me.

Where is Lowell though?

It feels like my body is empty and lighter than usual as I look around the swimming center. The pool water that was clear blue is now bright green and provides light to the dark room.

The smell of death fills the room. But I don't see anything here that would be dead.

Vines and shadows line the walls, causing the room to be overtaken with dead-looking plants, spikes, and monster-sized soot footmarks. This place is a haunted version of the swimming center but for some reason, it feels homey. The atmosphere is slightly warmer than the average classroom, but the temperature rapidly increases when I see a dark figure in the corner. I quickly stand up, hugging my back against the wall. Not taking my eyes off of it. It looks small in the distance but the closer it gets, the bigger it becomes.

An eleven-foot, lanky giant stands on the opposite side of the pool from me.

It seems similar to the creature I saw in the fire, and in our dorm unit earlier. Just without spikes covering the shoulders of this one. With no face and an all-black shadow appearance, I can't tell if it is staring at me or not. Looks as if this isn't their true form anyway.

I keep staring at it like I do when I see cockroaches in the corner of my room and just freeze there. The doors in the room are covered with vines so there is no way I can exit unless I rip them down.

All of a sudden, the creature motions his hand at me and points at the pool. My heart races as I slowly walk towards the pool, taking my eyes off of the creature for a second. Looking into the pool. There is nothing special about it, so I back up and look at the creature again. It is gone.

That's when I nervously turn around to see if it is behind me. But it has disappeared.

Walking towards the main entrance door so I can exit, someone walks in.

I quickly dart over to the wall, placing my hand on one of the vines by accident. The dark, lifeless color of the vines transfers onto my hand as pain courses up my arms. "Ouch!" I yell, pulling my hand off the vine. The part of the vine I had touched slowly starts turning green as if it is coming back to life. …*Which is not how life and death works. That's only in the movies and fantasy books,* I think to myself.

I slowly back up from the wall. Accidentally tripping over something while not paying attention.

My back then slams against the floor, as something hovers above me. It is a different shadow figure than the one that had disappeared earlier. This one has spikes.

I stand up and move over to the exit door just as it signs something. I'm not fluent in American sign language but I can identify certain words used to communicate. I was teaching myself but haven't practiced in years.

I think the figure can tell that I am clueless because it grabs my arm and drags me over to a wonky version of the storage closet. It throws me inside as I hear a click on the outside. Pain shoots through me as I land on my side but I get up, quickly running over to the door.

I jiggle the door trying to get out, but to no one's surprise… it is locked. I should have taken my chances with the non-spiked figure more than this one.

Looking around, the storage closet is dimly lit, and I can't see anything that could bring more light to this room. I lean my back against the door so that I can see all around the room.

Red curtains line the side of the room, making it look longer and tighter than before. A single body mirror at the far end of the wall catches my attention. I walk towards it.

The room gets darker the closer I get to the mirror and goes pitch black when I arrive at it. The only thing I can make out in the mirror is a person with their back turned to me. I touch the clear mirror with my hand and feel it go through. That's when I hear the door behind me creak open.

The presence of something huge towers over me. Is it a creature from before?

Not turning around, my heart beats through my throat.

They then pull me away from the mirror and I try to push them off. We both fall to the ground. Trying to crawl back to the mirror (still not looking at them), I feel their sharp nails slide into my legs. "Ahh!" I squeal, kicking them. Turning around with my back on the floor, looking at them.

The shadow has no spikes on it, but as we hold eye contact it starts to transform into a different look.

A scratch is noticeable on their face, they touch it lightly, then glance at the white blood on their soft, yellow-skinned fingers. "What are you?" I whisper, trying to squirm away.

Their eyes are gray and empty like their soul. But their face and body are gorgeous.

An evil goddess in disguise.

I scream while pulling my leg in the opposite direction. Their nails are still in my leg. Feels like knives. That's when they let go and climb on top of me. Their poisonous aura nearly steals the breath out of my lungs.

They reach out a finger and place it in the middle of my chest again.

I reach for one of the nearby curtains, pulling it as hard as I can. As it falls, the creature rolls off of me. Her dress flowing with her movement. The curtains fall on me.

Breathing heavily, I see something lift the other side of the curtain. Screaming, I crawl out of the other side as their feet step on the curtain. Trying to squish me under her size 14 feet.

Making it out of the other side, the creature throws something at the mirror. Breaking the top half of it. Glass falls at my feet as I turn around.

Taking a deep breath, I see her reflection through the bottom. She seems to be walking closer to me.

Quickly, I run over the glass as some of it painfully cuts into my feet. Taking my chances, I roll through the bottom of the mirror just as her hand grazes my hair.

I then see a small hand reaching out towards me. I grab it as they pull me out. It is soft, yet familiar.

I smile. I found her.

The last thing I hear is the creature let out a loud scream of anger: "NO!!! I NEED YOU!!"

I gasp for air, leaning over to cough out a ton of water.

Grabbing my chest in pain, the swim center lights shine bright. Blinding me at first. Richard jumps with fear at my sudden movement but then pulls me in close. Hugging me tightly.

"I died?" I ask as my chest throbs with pain.

He nods yes.

I try to catch my breath, whispering "shit" a few times in my head. Whatever that dream was, it was terrifying. 2/10, would not do again.

"Then why are you here? I told you to leave me," I sigh, slightly happy he's here.

He looked like he had been crying for a short while. I've never seen him cry before. *He's not, okay?,* I think to myself.

"I did leave while you were dead. And then Lowell passed out and your pulse came back," he pauses. "I didn't want to go against your wishes, and I promise I fought the urge to stay. But…I couldn't handle being away from you. And Lowell didn't make that shit easier."

I giggle, making no noise, thinking about ways that Lowell could have made it hard. She probably pushed him into a wall or something.

"You know, you make it so scary to love you. I can't say that I'm not happy to have come back to see you here," I smile, shaking my head.

Richard is still sitting on his butt while I stand above him. He then grabs my hand softly, pulls me down, and tilts my head down at him. Placing my hand against his chest for balance. Causing me to crouch down.

Our lips are nearly inches away.

"Listen, it hurt to be here."

"I'm sorry-"

"But I wouldn't want it any other way," he interrupts.

My eyes start to fill with tears as I glance at his lips before meeting his eyes again. His eyes still red.

"Show me that you wouldn't want me gone."

"Then stop telling me to leave, Xena"

"Then stop keeping secrets and pushing me away because you're too scared to cry."

"Then stop acting like you're too strong and when I'm there to protect you give me nothing!"

"Then want more for yourself you don't need me, Richard!"
"None of us need each other but I want you- I want you badly!"

His hand runs up the side of my face. His thumb on my cheek. I feel my heart skip and beat. I'm deeply flattered and surprised as his feelings towards me.

"I'm sorry I make it so hard for you to love me."

"Love is only hard because we chose not to communicate."

I place my hand on his. He faintly smiles, as his heart races faster.

"...I missed you so much," he replies, pushing my face softly to the side.

I smile and roll my eyes. My heart throbs as the tension rises in the room. It feels like the first day we meet but with less passion.

"Well, I was dead so I honestly can't say that I missed you too," I say, scrunching my nose.

He then breaks out laughing and kisses my forehead. I wipe it off, scrunching my nose again while laughing.

"I had the craziest dream," I whisper, looking down at my chest.

My face slowly turns red from realizing his soft lips kissed my forehead. Softer than most guys, to be honest.

There is a black colored mark on the middle of my chest that didn't exist there before. And there are cuts on my hands and feet.

Explaining my dream to Richard with a lot of hand motions, I put my shirt on to cover up my mark. I don't think Richard saw it because he said that he was sleeping when I came back to life. Also, he wasn't staring at my body when I was putting my shirt on or while talking to me.

He then told me about the new destination that a riddle told us to go to. So, I follow him out of the swimming center.

We walk and talk the whole way there. In the middle of it all, I pull out my phone and glance at the time, realizing that we only have about 6 hours left until sunrise.

You Know More Than You Claim {Lowell}

I jolt up, scaring Christopher who is sitting next to me. I am now sitting, leaning against the library wall.

The room is dark, lights flickering above. Wasn't I with Richard before this?

"Where's Richard?"

"After you fell out, he texted me, and we risked leaving both of you to switch rooms. I wanted to be with you, and even though Richard was fighting it, he wanted to be with Xena since her pulse came back."

I smile. I'm glad he went back to her. She needs him more than I ever will, and he needs her more than he'll express.

My chest is pounding with pain.

My back hurts too.

Christopher then places his hand on my neck as if he is checking my pulse. He sighs a sigh of relief as his phone then falls out of his pocket.

"How long was I out?"

"Probably twenty minutes since it's only 11:40. This is your second time passing out, are you okay?"

"From my knowledge, yes," I shrug.

Just as he helps me off the floor slowly, Richard and Xena bust through the library door, closing it behind them. It's strange how unbothered we all are about this. It's like our personalities switched once the game started.

Like this never-ending traumatic experience has only made us more vulnerable and closer as a group than we would have ever been without it.

I watch as Christopher speed-walks to one of the tables in the middle of the library. He cuts on the lights, causing the bookshelves that line the walls to be seen more easily. In confusion, the three of us walk over to Christopher and lean over the table.

Xena and I quickly hug as a smile spreads on both of us because we most definitely missed each other.

However, she seems off.

We sit down as Christopher ransacks the shelves looking for something. When he comes back over to us, he lays down a note for the rest of us to read.

You work quicker than I thought
So you have more than enough time
Find your prize here
To end the game before sunrise
...don't forget to look closely at the darkness
It will come to bite one of you

I smile after reading it, since this is the last clue card and all we have to do is find a prize. I'm hopeful that no task cards come up again because those are worse than the clue ones.

Thinking to myself, I yawn and run my hands through my hair.

My body then shivers hard. I realize that my pants are still soaked from diving. Regardless of being wet and cold, my torso is mostly dry, so I'm not too worried. Though I would like to dry off at some point.

"So, what's the plan, Richard? I know something's on your mind," Xena asks, breaking the silence.

"Christopher and Xena will go look on one side of the library and Lowell and I on the other. If we find something interesting, then we can call each other over."

"Sounds good," Xena yawns.

Her yawn causes a chain reaction in the rest of us, making all of us yawn too. I know that the closer we get to sunrise the harder it will be to stay awake. Looking around the table, I have a gut feeling that the boys will be keeping Xena and I awake as time progresses.

We sit there, staring in silence, waiting for someone to get up and start the plan. Separating, even in smaller groups, can still cause us to get picked off.

I then give Richard a look and he gets up. Following behind him rolling my eyes, Richard and I walk away from the others.

Humming to myself, we head through the aisles to the back of the library. He's walking fast like he knows where he is going. It takes a few minutes before we see a door. Barricaded with wood planks over it.

Confused, he smiles at me and looks at the door.

"You knew this was here, didn't you?" I ask.

"No, not exactly. The location was just a guess."

"Okay. Say I decide to believe that. Why plan to be with me?"

"Because you're less likely to care if I said I knew what was inside," he shrugs, pulling something out of his backpack.

It's a tiny crowbar that I don't remember him putting inside. Helping him, we both take the millions of nails out of the boards. Remaining quiet.

After a few minutes, we finally get all the boards and nails off.

Coming across a locked door, Richard rolls his eyes, upset, and calls for the others to come over to our side of the library.

We can hear them walking and talking over towards us as we continue sitting on the floor.

"What's keeping me from telling the others that you know more than you're telling us?" I whisper, staring at the lock.

He smirks, sizing me up.

"Don't question my motives. I'm the biggest thing that can help us live, unless you want to die?"

"Don't threaten my life," I snicker. "If I die, we all die. Real question is, do *you* want to die? Cause I'm not scared to die at the hands of you."

Richard then laughs in amusement and holds out his hand saying, "Point made."

Rolling my eyes and faintly smiling. He's so annoying, I see why Christopher has a hard time talking to him.

Locked Away Stories {Richard}

As we wait for the other two to show up, I kick the wooden planks to the side. Giving us more space. Lowell looks at me, acting more like we found this and not as if we were intentionally looking for it. Doing the same, the others finally show up. We all stand up, huddling around the door. Christopher nor Xena question the findings of this door.

"The door is locked but we think that the prize could be behind it. The only issue is that we need someone to pick the lock," I announce, glancing at Lowell.

She just rolls her eyes and crouches in front of the huge red velvet door. We keep quiet as she runs her hands over both locks. Examining how to open them. She then laughs, lets air out of her nose in amusement, and shakes her head before staring back at us.

"With two vintage keyhole locks and no door handle, it should take me about ten minutes to unlock this door. I just need a bobby pin or a knife," she shrugs.

"Okay," Xena replies, wiping off the end of her pocketknife before handing it to Lowell. Facing the handle at her.

"Here."

Christopher and I look at each other, then at the girls, and then back at each other. Shrugging, impressed.

Sitting on the ground against the wall next to Lowell, Christopher and Xena are talking about sharks. Which breed is stronger and what they would do if they ran into one. I'm just scrolling through my phone and typing poetry in my notepad for what feels like ten minutes before Lowell taps my shoulder. Her smile widens as her gaze darts to Xena before she looks at the door again. With cold hands, she stands up and motions for me to help her open the door.

It is heavier than we expected so, Xena and Christopher come over and join us. As we finally pull it open, I nearly fall to the ground. Thankfully, I just crashed into Christopher, who is standing up behind me.

Awkwardness spreads when he looks at me though. His hands are on my hips to help me brace myself, and my leg is in between both of his legs. He smiles, asking if I'm okay. His smile is so annoying.

Quickly looking away, all four of us peek into the room. There is a single book in the middle of the floor that looks like it has been through some things.

As the rest of us hold the door open, not moving, Christopher goes in and grabs the book. Closing the door behind him.

The four of us then head back to the table, placing the book in the center while we all stand on one side. The book is called "Crystal View," so it must contain information and the history of our town. Flipping to the table of contents, a section about curses catches my eye, so I go to that page.

Nothing.

We skim through the pages that are talking about golden birthdays, creature sights, missing kids, and the town overall. All the things that outsiders would say are scary or dangerous, while our townspeople see it as normal.

"Richard, you are flipping the pages too fast. Are you even comprehending what it says, because I only understand half," Christopher asks, placing his hand in the middle of the book so that I can't flip anymore.

We handle the book with care due to the brown, frail pages and dust that sits on the cover.

"Sorry, I read fast. But yes, I do understand what's going on. It's talking about when golden birthdays started, and the first person who died. Her name was Obeah Green."

We all sit in the chairs as Xena pushes the book closer to me. They must want me to summarize what the book is talking about, so I open it and flip to the page. The only issue I have with this situation is that the book was trapped inside of a door, which makes me feel like we shouldn't be reading this. Like once we open this, it will stir up more trouble than needed.

"You know I never really liked calling this creature a creature or a figure. It makes it seem like it has no personality or life story. But then again, I didn't read the pages while we were flipping through, so I could have missed it," Lowell mentions while putting her head down.

"The creature is a male and his name is Kindal Stewart. The book explains that he was born a twin. His twin sister's name is Ziona Stewart. It says that he died soon after birth and that there is no further information on his sister's life," I answer.

"Can you please repeat those names?"

I pause, trying to think of how I said it the first time so I can say it slower. I fear saying it too many times because of the evil meanings.

"Kindal is the male twin and Zee-o-na is the female twin. The book explains that Kindal is the reason why our golden birthdays are the way they are. Though I don't know where his sister fits into the situation."

"Okay. So, is that all those pages explain or is there more? Like why does he make our golden birthdays a life or death game?"

"I don't know. The only thing the book confirms is that thousands of kids have gone missing since this whole thing started 30 years ago around 1990. But most of the pages on golden birthdays are just fluffed and repeated," I shrug.

"So, if it started in 1990, they would have been born around 1968 if they died at 22?" Lowell asks.

"Well, in order to do that, they would have to know what the afterlife would bring them to, right? They would have had to know how to kill or how to find people long before they started," Xena adds.

Lowell shrugs in agreement and looks at us boys to see what we think. They are bouncing ideas off of each other.

"I do agree with you Lowell and Xena; you do have a point. Speaking of the fact that we know little about their life, it's safe to assume that once they died, they probably didn't immediately start killing people. So, I would assume they worked up their plan for a few years and were born within the window of-"

"The 1950s. A time where life was more violent, turbulent, and more segregated. Aside from the more colorful events," Christopher interrupts, with his annoying smile.

I feel my face slightly getting hot at his annoying smile.

"Oh, someone pays attention to history. I find that class to be a snoozefest," Lowell teases, fake snoring.

Xena and I laugh as Christopher rolls his eyes in amusement.

"Of course, you do. You always ask me for my notes."

"Wait, you take notes?" Xena says jokily. "Definitely slide them my way too, then. That class is hard."

"You sit right next to me and have never failed a test. You don't need my notes."

"Correct, but if you keep using your hand to cover your answers then I'll actually have to study," she says.

Christopher laughs and says, "Fine, I'll give you my notes to study."

I raise an eyebrow.

"Well, since you're helping people out…" I shrug.

He laughs.

"We might as well just study together. I need help in math anyway," he looks at Lowell.

We all then look at each other and laugh in agreement, joking around.

Thinking back to the golden birthday of the information we already know; I try to think about why Kindal would want to kill people on their birthdays. Maybe it has something to do with the mark I've had on my chest since I was 15.

But I can't bring that up with the others. They probably won't understand what I mean.

After a while of thinking, spacing out from reality, I realize that Xena and Lowell are resting.

Xena closed her eyes first. Lowell takes a while to close hers. Even then, Lowell is not fully asleep because she keeps randomly opening her eyes, checking on Xena. But doesn't move enough to wake her up.

Xena's head lies on top of Lowell's hand while her arm is over her back. Her curls are spread softly across her arm as Lowell lays her head on Xena's shoulder while facing her head towards Xena.

Adorable, I think to myself while glancing at Christopher. He gets up abruptly, tears in his eyes, as if a thought in his head worked him up.

That's when he disappears from view.

"Could there be three creatures?" Lowell yawns, not even opening her eyes.

"I doubt it, but maybe," I say, distracted.

Looking into the direction Christopher went. Looking back at Lowell, she seems to have fallen asleep again and hasn't heard a word I said.

I glance over at the clock, realizing that we have time to spare. Everyone in this group is so emotionally unstable. Makes me think that

Lowell is the sanest one of us all. But then again, I haven't seen her crash yet.

Eww.

I shake at that thought.

Getting up quietly, I walk in the direction Christopher went. Towards the bookshelves.

Peaking my head down two aisles, I walk down the third one. Christopher is sitting against the bookshelf. Head looking up at the ceiling. Thank goodness he's not crying because I suck at comforting people when they're crying.

"Christopher?" I say, standing a little ways away from him. He looks up at me.

"You okay?"

"Sure," he says, looking the other way.

"You know, leaving can make you an easier target. It's best if you don't separate from the group."

"Oh, now you care about that. Nearly an hour ago, you were ready to ditch your friend," he replies in an angered tone.

"You're right. I don't even know why I bothered coming over here."

I walk out of the aisle to join the girls. Luckily, they are still there sleeping because I couldn't forgive myself if they got killed. A second time at that.

As I walk towards the table, I feel something grab my wrist. Pulling me into the first aisle closest to the table. Their hands cover my mouth, so I bite their fingers hard. Causing them to let me go.

"Ouch," Christopher says, shaking his hand up and down.

"What the hell? What's your problem?" I say, pushing him.

He stumbles, but doesn't fall to the floor.

"I don't know. You're the one walking around here alone knowing that we need to stay together."

"Says the one who left the table to soak in their misery. I only got up to make sure you were okay."

His eyes grow wide.

"Seriously?" he says, with sad puppy eyes.

"Oh, don't do this to me. You know I could care less about you."

"Aww," he then hugs me and rocks me side to side with pure enjoyment.

I push him off as he laughs.

"Seriously though, I remained at the table. I was there the whole time. Right across from you but you seemed like you were following something."

"I was following…you," I say slowly.

Scared that I was seeing things.

Christopher smiles.

"I am playing with you. That was me the whole time. Just wanted to take the opportunity to scare you," he laughs.

I then roll my eyes and peer through the bookshelf at the girls. They're still sleeping.

"Don't do that again," I squint my eyes. "No more separating."

"You are so uptight. I just needed to clear my head."

He sits on the ground. I crouch next to him.

"What's up then?"

"Me?" He immediately asks, like I didn't just ask him a question.

"Yes, you."

"Oh, nothing."

"Man, stop wasting time and tell me what's wrong. I hardly wanna help you out, but I'm tryna get back to solving riddles."

He sighs, running his right hand through his hair. I nudge him on the shoulder.

"I just feel like I'm trying too hard to keep everyone together. That even in the end you all will end up leaving anyways and the group will split up."

I laugh at his corny response, then clear my throat as he glares at me like *Shut up*.

"Sorry, but that could never be the case. If anything, you are keeping us together. Balancing us out emotionally and making sure we don't leave anyone behind. None of us are leaving, even the ones who died. If that is the case at the end of the game."

"Perhaps."

He pauses, looking at the girls through the bookshelf.

I don't know if he can feel it, but every time I look at those two, it's like passion fills the air. And not the toxic love kind. But they're not even close like that. I personally wish I had someone who made me feel safe and needed, excluding Xena. Someone I can risk it all for and be more than a friend with.

"They are cute. Except for the fact that seeing them makes you think anyone nearby could love you," Christopher laughs, glancing into my eyes.

My heart skips a beat as I avoid smiling.

"Thank you, Richard!"

"For what?"

"For following me back here."

"Yeah, mhm. Just don't make it a habit," I say, holding my hand out to help him up.

____ We walk over to the girls and act as if nothing happened.

Xena slowly opens her eyes and looks up at us. Christopher starts to yawn.

I ask them if they were listening to what was going on earlier about the book. Not that I truly care. It is half-past twelve and they are going to have to stay awake if we're going to finish this game.

Or at least Lowell has to.

"Yes, I was paying attention to what you said. I was just thinking about the whole situation and I got tired," she yawns.

Stretching some as Lowell ducks under her arm so it won't hit her.

"Sorry, Lowell. Oh, and to be honest I can probably find the spot…in the book that may mention something about his life. That should explain why he does this," Xena yawns again, shaking her curls back out.

Lowell rubs her eyes, yawning too.

"Here," Christopher says, sliding the book over from me to her.

His eyes locking onto mine as his face turns slightly red around his cheeks. I try not to look at his enticing pink lips. I need to get away from these two girls. The energy in the air is too sweet.

Lowell then hits my shoulder for no reason, breaking the tension. Xena grabs the book loudly and begins flipping through the book pages.

She stops and rips out a loose page in the back of the book. Skimming over it quickly.

Xena shows us the page while also summarizing it.

"I found a news article from ten years ago that talks about a reopened case. Their grandma had made an entry to the local newspaper thirty years ago before she died. Grandma Zira's side of the story was that her grandson Kindal, or K, is what she called him, was bullied. Abused all his life…but the newspaper said that the grandma was deranged, prone to lying, and died five years before her grandson's golden birthday at 22," she pauses.

"I'm guessing they didn't trust her. Was there a reason?" Richard asks.

"They interviewed his mom and she said she never had twins. She claims she only had a daughter which was ruled out because there was a child's room upstairs." She yawns again, causing me to yawn too. Then clears her throat.

"So then why are they talking about the boy and not the girl? They're painting him out as the main one yet this news article was ten years ago," Lowell asks.

"Well, I don't know. All the reopened case says is that there were masculine clothes hanging up in the closet and a bunk bed. The mom had a weak alibi for the bed and the clothes but the case was dropped. It was like the kid never existed. This wasn't the full case file so I don't fully know what happened. Though he wasn't talked about for a few years."

Christopher then slides us a black and white image from the book. It's covered in dried blood and shows three people under it. The girl's face is scratched out and so are the boys'.

She then adds, "And it would have stayed that way had his sister not spoken up about his existence when she was 22. Her twin brother had died playing a game on their golden birthday, March 22nd. Then days later, Ziona died due to an unknown reason and the mom disappeared after she burned her house and the evidence down. No one's body was found."

"Wow," the three of us say simultaneously.

We are speechless at how fast she found that. And about the news article.

Left intrigued as I now want to know where his mother went, where the original case is, and how he died. It feels like a mystery that we have to solve in order to release these creatures' souls from the earth.

I look at my phone and grab the book. I have always wondered why you can't text people during your golden birthday unless they are playing the game with you.

Using my scarf to cover the mysterious mark on my chest, I wave Christopher over.

I carry the book as he follows me to the room. Inserting one of the wooden planks through a space at the bottom door so it won't close. Christopher walks inside the room. Placing the book back onto the stand. He looks around for a moment. I find myself slightly walking in as he starts to walk out.

There are five passages and doors that one could go through. They could be other entrances or just dead ends.

As I look at the painted gray walls and red carpet, I see something in the corner of my eye. A woman stands there. She's peeking through one of the doors while staring at us. She is an old, skinny, white woman that looks like she could be blown away by a small gust of wind. Her scary red eyes pierce into my soul but just as I back up away from her, I bump into Christopher.

I think to myself *Why is he always the first thing I crash into?,* while positioning my body next to him. Nervous, and trying not to startle him, I turn his head to look at the woman.

But once he looks, the woman disappears.

Darting into the dark.

"Who was that?"

"I don't know," my voice shakes, "Let's just leave."

He nods his head as we walk out of the door.

Quickly closing it behind us.

Lustful Explorations {Lowell}

Richard and Xena suggested that we split up in groups of two and look for more information on the game. See if we run across clues since we have to find the prize and the clue card was no help. So, I suggested going with Xena and him with Christopher.

Richard gets on my nerves but since we are just looking around, I'd rather not spend my time with him. Especially since Christopher is growing more of a liking towards him and Xena doesn't care either way.

Now with Xena out of my sight, I decide to examine the books to see if my favorite one is here. When I approach the end of the aisle, I see the book and grab it. I am giddy with happiness while I look for Xena so I can show her the book.

Beaming with a huge smile over my face, it stops when my eyes lock onto her.

She is leaning against the wall, reading a book. A sad expression across her face, but underneath is an intriguing faint smile that is breathtaking. As she looks up from the book, glancing around, I duck behind the bookshelf so she won't see me. Then peek back to look at her as she looks back down at the book.

Her pointer finger lightly runs across the page while she gently grips the book. I think to myself, *I could watch her all night,* but not in a stalkerish way. It's just that she's so gentle with everything she does that if it were me, I'd be lost in her touch. Staring at her makes my heart and brain paint a future with her. One filled with success, marriage, and possible kids.

I sigh and try to shake off the feeling. It feels so random, I didn't know I felt that way.

My heart throbs with pain as a tear falls from Xena's face. She looks hurt, yet her smile widens. It's like her face is showing the pain I'm feeling right now. Not her actually being in pain.

My body then goes light as my face turns red. Causing my grip to loosen on the book I am holding.

It loudly collides with the ground. Both of us jump, startled. She glances at me sharply before sighing.

"Oops," I say, nervously laughing.

A headache forming.

Xena starts laughing while I nervously struggle to pick the book up. When I finally get the book off the floor, I lean against the wall, trying to play it off cool. She then walks over and stands in front of me. Her book is still in her hand.

"I think you're picking up on my clumsy behavior," she teases, touching the book in my hands.

Her hand grazes mine slightly, causing me to accidentally jump. Dropping it again.

"I guess that's what I get for being around you so much," I tease back, leaving it there. She is still reading that same page in the book.

"Is that page really that good?"

"Oh," she says, not realizing how long she was reading it. "Yeah, well, not really. It's just cute. One of those scenes that make you fantasize about being in a relationship."

She then closes it, walking over to the shelf. Placing it gently back where she got it from.

The lights are dim in the back of the library and flicker softly without going completely off for too long.

As she walks back towards me, I think romantic thoughts, but try to brush them off.

While walking along the library walls, we both hear a low growl in the distance behind us. The lights above us flicker faster, and we stop in place. My heart races as she motions me to keep walking slowly. There is a door a few feet to the right of us in the far corner. Though if we make any sudden moves the thing behind us could attack us.

Creeping towards the door, the growl grows closer to us. Louder as the footsteps hit the floor.

I think this thing is following us.

Xena and I slowly creep past two bookshelves, hugging the walls in silence.

But we are three aisles away from reaching the door. Hopefully it opens.

Sighing, I tighten my grip on her hand and we run towards the door we were aiming for. Passing three aisles as fast as we can as the creature chases us. Never once do we look back.

Twisting the handle, it's unlocked, thankfully. We run inside the dark room, not thinking much of it.

Xena squeezes my hand hard while we pull the door closed. The animal scratches the wall.

"Ouch, ouch, ouch," I repeat, shaking off her hand.

Rubbing my now sore hand.

Pulling out her phone, she cuts on her flashlight before entering behind me. Pointing at the ceiling to illuminate the room.

"Sorry. I'm scared of the dark."

Looking around, we see two handicapped bathroom stalls along the right side and a light switch next to us. Sinks on the back wall with urinals and dividers to part them. I flick the switch and look around at the lines of blood on the sink and walls. White stains on the floor and toilets. Xena investigates the broken mirror for a moment before looking at the boys' urinals. Even though it's usually not bloody, she seems to not have been in a boy's bathroom before.

"You good?" I ask, as she peeks her head out of the bathroom stall.

Walking out of it.

"Yeah, I've just never seen a bathroom so…disgusting. It's weird because I don't recall anyone coming in here."

"Well, obviously you haven't cleaned the club's bathroom on a Saturday Buzz night," I joke.

She laughs at me, rolling her eyes.

"Oh, please. Try cleaning the girl's bathroom after Friday Freak night."

I laugh at her while walking towards the back of the bathroom near the urinals. Xena rolls her sleeve back and pulls out a note in the back crack of one of the broken urinals.

She reads:

Two lost girls
In a boy's restroom
Now all you need to do is clean up my mess
Maybe you will find an answer to your quest
But don't fret, you can skip the urinals

CLINK *CLANK*...the sound of a few cleaning bottles hitting the floor. We look behind us. Then on the floor. Then at each other.

"Seriously? We have to clean the bathroom now."

"Well, look on the bright side - at least the note wasn't around a wolf's neck," I shrug.

Xena blinks her eyes twice, annoyed, puts two gloves on, and grabs a spray bottle. The only thing I'm assuming we are cleaning is the sink, mirror, floor, and walls. Proceeding to do the same, she starts spraying the wall.

I work on the sink.

"Happy Birthday, Lowell. I feel like I should say it before it actually ends," Xena says out of nowhere.

"Thank you! You're the only one to say that all night," I reply.

"Oh?"

"Yeah, but it's understandable. Half of us died, and the rest of us are trying not to die again. If I was in y'all's position, I wouldn't say it. There's nothing happy about this birthday," I laugh.

I'm happy that she said it though. Aside from this birthday, I haven't been wished a happy birthday on my actual birthday in years. Not even a happy early birthday. Even Xena was the first person to say happy early birthday, aside from Christopher.

It grows silent as she looks at me with sad eyes before looking away.

"Are you in a relationship?" I ask while scrubbing the walls. She continues wiping off the bloodstains on the sink.

"No," she answers, not looking in my direction as she's too focused on cleaning. "Do I rub off as being in one?"

"Kind of. It's like you're either in one or you were in a bad one and are no longer looking to date. A woman like you would get people left and right, but as you said in the closet, you keep rejecting them."

"Are you stalking my life?" She jokes. I smile.

"No, I just got out of a toxic relationship. Just trying to better me before I get into another one and I guess I'm just trying to find someone to relate too," I say, raising my shirt to cover my nose from breathing in the toxic fumes. She looks at me and smiles, before looking away.

"Well looks like you found someone. I did too… and I also got a mark on my chest after I drowned," she says, pointing at me.

I look into the mirror and stare at it. It's a huge black mark over my chest. Sore to the touch.

Xena wipes off the now clean wall. Cutting on the fan in the room next to the light switch before spraying down the mirror.

"I'll ask Richard about the marks later. I think he could explain it. He has a way with words," Xena says, looking back at my mark.

Then at my eyes.

"Yeah- seems like the type of guy who would talk you through it" I wink.

"Chile-"Xena laughs at me, flustered and throws her wet, nasty rag on my shoulder. I throw it back at her.

"What you didn't deny it."

I raise an eyebrow at her. Maybe she doesn't see what I see in his eyes when he looks at her or talks about her. She cleans the mirror, scooting closer to me as I clean the counter next to her. She reaches on her tippy toes to get the top.

"Have you ever talked about your emotions for each other?" I ask, looking at her.

She stops wiping the top and looks at me. Raising an eyebrow.

"Lowell, what are you getting at?"

"Nothing, it's just something I see between you. Like y'all have history."

"If you want to know how we met you could just ask. I wouldn't give you an answer - but you can just ask. We've had history, yes, but don't read into it, we're just friends," she replies.

Getting off her tippy toes, nearly sliding on the water on the ground she says "Ouch!" while placing her hand on my shoulder to brace herself. I hold her with my hand as she pulls her shoes off. Something must have struck her inside it.

"Fine. I guess I can believe you."

"You don't have to," she says, looking at my mark again. I don't mind her glancing - it is different and stands out on my body.

"But I guess- as my friend now, of course, I can tell you that he is a good guy to be with if you're curious," she teases, nudging me.

Touching my mark by accident.

I wince, then reply, "Oh, eww no," while fake gagging, "I respect him but he's not my type."

"Hey, woman to woman I don't care if you go after my best friend, he's not my possession. ~~He might need that openness too~~," she trails off on the end making it hard for me to understand her.

She quickly moves her hand from me and apologizes for causing me pain. Saying she didn't mean to cross boundaries, before asking me another question.

"So, you're not together. What do you want if we make it out of this game?" I question. She looks at me as her eyes slowly light up.

"I'm going to a famous artist. Like Claude Monet. And before you say anything about how it's difficult and you're shooting too high in a world that doesn't care anymore- I'm going to have my paintings pay my bills."

She looks at me, then puts her rag down.

"I wasn't going to shoot your ideas down, I'm chasing dreams of making music, I understand the struggle. Do you want your own studio?"

"More than anything. My own little space with a personal mural on the roof and dried watercolors staining the walls," she smiles. "You sing?"

"Yes, but I produce- well at least I'm trying too. It's hard to find clients and an audience."

"Well, I believe you'll find it! Passion from a struggling artist only dies when we decide to let the world tell us no."

I hold out my hand.

She looks at me for a few seconds before she places hers on top. Her palm to the sky. I move her hand closer to my chest as she stops it before touching my skin.

Xena whispers, smiling, "Don't tell anyone but I entered a big art contest. A cash prize and putting my piece in a museum."

"Well, you should let me see it, I'd love to know your style," I whisper back.

"I have a photo I can show you."

"That… or we can see it on the museum wall."

"Alright," she smiles as her eyes dart to something behind me. "I missed a spot."

I glance back and see a blood stain we overlooked. Xena slowly steps closer. Directly in front of me, accidentally placing her ice-cold hands on my chest while reaching above me.

After a few seconds, the world slowly grows dark.

It feels like I'm falling into an endless black pit. Able to see nothing. I try to scream on the inside. No sound comes out.

I'm scared, yet feel oddly in power. *Xena!,* I try to yell as I fall in the dark. I then forcibly stop moving and hit the ground softly. No response from Xena. No sound comes out of my mouth. My ears then pick up a voice.

"L-Lowell, please!" a voice moans softly, sounding as if they're having trouble breathing. I feel scratching on my right arm but I see no one around. Suddenly something pushes me onto the floor. I fall forwards, using my arms to prevent myself from falling on my face. Letting out a quick scream as something scratches down into my back.

"Stop, stop, please, you're moving too fast," the voice cries. That's when something sharp pokes onto my stomach. "I don't want to hurt you."

I look around scared, calling Xena's name a few more times but not able to make a sound come out. As I turn around, a cold hand runs over one of my eyes. "Xena?" I sigh. It uncovers my eye.

My heart races fast. As I see broken pieces of glass on the floor in front of me. There is a lavender glow shining through it. Picking a piece of glass up, I peer through and see a faint purple body dart behind me. Looking behind me, nothing's there but pitch-black darkness.

Glancing back into the glowing glass, I see the face of the creature who marked me before. They grin before covering my head in a bag. Wrapping their hands over my waist with their other hand.

My heart skips beats.

Before I know it, my body goes flying in the air.

Lights from the bathroom hit my eyes.

As I rub my eyes, I notice that I am laying on top of Xena, pinning her to the wall. She pushes me off, struggling, and quickly stands in front of me as if she is looking for something. Someone.

My eyes are still trying to adjust as she coughs hard, struggling for air.

I struggle to stand up, but I remain quiet as she walks around with her bloody knife. Checking each bathroom stall before looking at me. She walks over and leans in closer to my face, never breaking eye contact, as fear courses through me.

I step back one more time as she points her knife at me.

"Move and I kill you," she says in a deep yet stern tone, pointing her knife at me.

I'm slightly attracted as she is rubbing her neck.

I don't make a sound as she looks at me angrily, but my eyes stare back at her confused. I don't remember ever being on top of her. From the looks of it, she was fighting something and when I was thrown into whatever dark pit I was in, I landed on her.

"Give me my friend back!" she yells, then threatens, "Or you'll never s-survive."

Xena coughs and softly cries as she looks at me. Blood on her knife. Pain in her eyes. Her body looks like it is going to collapse from exhaustion.

Biting my lip, I try not to tear up from her tearing up. My heart races faster by the second.

"ANSWER ME!"

"I don't know what to say. You're trying to KILL ME," I reply, confused.

Her right leg then goes out and she falls to the floor, crashing onto her knee. Her blade is still gripped tightly in her hand, ready for if she needs to use it again. I cover my hand with my face, moving over to her to see if she's okay.

"Xena, I-" I mumble.

"Stop!" she says, with pure terror in her voice.

Walking over to me, she then sizes me up like a caveman and cuts lightly into my forearm.

"Ouch!" I say, as she pushes me and puts her knife to my neck, with her face to my ear.

Out of fear, I push her into the wall, grabbing her knife with my hand. Screaming as the blade cuts into my palm and she pulls it back. Pressing it on my neck again, blood drips down while she uses her free hand to pin down my arm above my head.

Her grip is amazing in a scary, dominant way.

Preparing to die at the hand of someone I have known for less than two weeks, she stops pressing down.

I open one of my eyes. The room grows incredibly dark, as a few drops of blood come from her hand.

Both of my eyes then grow wide, as the creature who marked me before stands in front of Xena.

All Xena does is smile at the creature. One of Xena's eyes slowly turns grey, like the emptiness of someone's soul. She looks slightly confused but stands up in front of me as my creature towers over her.

Xena stares into the creature's ice-cold eyes with no fear.

How is she not scared?

Xena then takes a deep breath, saying sharply, "Leave her with me."

My creature lets out a manly laugh of amusement that almost makes me laugh. She steps closer to Xena. Xena steps back slightly and moves against the wall. Causing her to glance at me before looking back at the creature. But my creature stares at her, grinning.

"*It hadn't crossed my mind that after our last interaction, minutes ago, you would want to see me so soon.*"

Xena doesn't respond as my creature looks at me, then back at her. The ghost creature, for once, actually looks like she has remorse for us. As if she feels emotions.

The ghost lady places her finger under Xena's left eye, the one that Xena doesn't know is grey and sighs. Xena doesn't move. She continues to stand in front of me. Guarding me.

"*You are just like her. Or - at least how she used to be,*" my creature frowns, glancing away at the bathroom door. "*But you will never win.*"

The creature looks at Xena with angered eyes. Her brows grow inward, and hair starts to float some. She then yells a screeching battle cry and pulls her hand back. Aiming to hit Xena.

I quickly grab Xena's hand and pull her down fast as she screams. Wrapping my hand around her head as she falls to the ground, slightly under me now.

The ghost lady's hand hits the wall. Once it makes an impact she disappears into thin air. Leaving a black soot mark on the wall next to us.

Xena lays her head in my chest, curling her body against mine, as part of her side is on the floor. Looking around, I tell her it's fine as she opens her eyes. Her eyes focus on the black soot mark immediately.

Moving off of her, we sit on the nasty floor, terrified, before standing up. Examining the soot mark, she stands to watch the door behind me to make sure nothing comes up behind us as I face the wall.

"It's nothing. Just a burn mark," I say, looking back at her.

Xena's shaking slightly and covering her left ear with her hand. Tears in her eyes but none have fallen. I grab her hand and she jumps lightly. Looking at me, then our intertwined hands, before squeezing my hand tightly.

I then let go out of anger.

"Why did you try to kill me?"

"I'm so sorry I put a knife to your neck! I figured that if I tried to kill you then one of the creatures would show up again. She looks different in comparison to the one that marked me."

Xena pauses, rubbing her left ear, then looking at the small amount of blood on it as she moves her hand.

"I didn't realize how strong you are."

She must be referring to when I pushed her.

"I accept your apology, but if you do that again, can you warn me? I didn't mean to push you that hard, but I was scared," I smile.

Knowing that I would let this goddess of a woman step on me if she wanted to, I can't bear the idea of hurting her. She smiles and nods.

"I don't care about the blood, don't apologize. It's not the worst thing that's happened in the past few minutes. I only care about you. Are you fine now that you're back?" Xena asks worriedly.

Touching under both of my eyes and moving my head slightly to see my neck. I don't know much she knows or even how she spawned the creature first. Xena has bruises on her neck and hands, along with blood on her arms, but she doesn't care about her bruises. She only cares about mine.

"I'm fine. I just don't remember how all this happened. One moment you were touching my mark, and in the next everything blacked out. All I could hear was screaming and something scratched me before I was supposedly thrown into you. And then I woke up, kinda, and it took a minute for my eyes to adjust but-," I rant fast, hardly making any sense.

Xena just smiles in relief as a tear falls down her face. I stop talking, worried that she is crying because of me. I back up some from her as she wipes her face, sniffling now.

Before I can say anything else, I pull her into my arms. She gives into the huge hug while crying, "I fought so hard to get you back. I thought I lost you."

Taken aback, I stiffen up.

She continues hugging me over the shoulders while her hands shake.

I slowly hug her back around her waist, more confused than ever. It feels like my heart is growing softer from those words. But as I rub her back and bury my face in her shoulder, I can't help but feel happier that she didn't let me die at the hands of this creature. She even went as far as to tell the creature to back off of me while also trying to get me to not kill her.

That's when I break down in our silence. Crying as if this is the last time I will be able to cry.

She holds me closely, rubbing my back with soft hands.

Roll The Ads {Christopher}

We walk around the library for an hour looking for the prize and reading fiction books. All of us are getting tired, but it's obvious that I must stay awake for the others. We only have about four hours left of the game.

As of right now, I am standing next to Xena. Looking at a book that Lowell gave us. It is a romantic tale with genuine circumstances about characters that make the book controversial and sad, yet so empowering for individuals like us. Us being people that work at that bar because our queer ways don't "fit" into this homophobic town.

With all things considered, I have not perused the book personally. I'm just going off what the summary on the back makes it seem like. Lowell has read it and highly recommends it so maybe I will read it soon. *"That is if we can get out of this game,"* I frown, glancing around this dimly lit room.

Getting my focus back on the game, there is no sign of a prize in this library, and my stomach is growling loudly. I almost forgot that I have not eaten since yesterday morning.

"Christopher," Lowell sings from the table.

She and Richard are sitting down at the table, so Xena and I head over to them. Walking slowly, Xena looks back at me for the fourth time in the past five minutes.

Leaning over the table, holding my aching stomach, Lowell stares back and forth between us two with a concerned, protective momma bear look.

"So…Richard and I were talking about taking a break from the game to eat. The cafeteria is still open so we can raid the fridge or something," Lowell smiles.

"Okay, but I'll prepare the food. You guys look like you are about to fall asleep," I respond.

"Thank you!"

We head out of the library, quickly. Towards the cafeteria on the east wing. There is no excitement between us and everything remains dark on our way there. I suggested that we use a flashlight, but we ran out of batteries a long time ago. Richard confirmed that.

Once we arrive, Lowell and Richard sit down at one of the tables, so I head straight to the kitchen. Xena follows me.

The cafeteria door slams closed, causing a loud thud to echo through the place. All of us jump at first. I look at Xena. She seemed unbothered, like she didn't hear it. Or more like she didn't pay enough attention to it.

That's a first.

Cutting on a light, we look around.

The kitchen is magnificent. Rosewood cabinets, a double oven, and granite countertops. Along with a little window cut out above the sink. It surprises me. A kitchen like this in a college cafeteria feels enchanting, but when you think about it, this college isn't like normal colleges. We can do almost anything we want here, and the tuition is lower than low. Practically free for residents because of how "haunted" this town is.

Taking two frozen bags from the fridge, I begin preheating the oven and getting to work. Glancing at Xena as she sits on the counter humming and swinging her feet back and forth. She stares at the floor with a lost expression on her face.

"Is something troubling you?"

She looks up from the ground, making eye contact with me. I must have caught her off guard. She now has a surprised expression, along with a nervous one. I want to assume that this is about Lowell but with Xena's bold yet innocent personality, it could be anything.

"Umm…I was thinking about who is going to fill DJ's spot at work," she shrugs. "Keeps my focus off the game."

"What do you mean? We only have one DJ?"

"Well, he was offered a record deal so he could kick off his music. His last shift is tomorrow after Lowell's birthday is over. I thought you knew that," she replies, biting her lip.

Nervously looking at me, while her eyes dart left to right for a second.

"No. I have known him for so long and he still did not tell me. It is fine, I guess."

Overwhelming sadness settles in my heart as I lean over the counter. I care about him and I do not want him to go, but we always knew he would follow his dreams and leave this town. My sadness just comes from the fact that he did not tell me that he was leaving so soon. There is so much I wanted to say to him. So many things I wish we could have done.

"I'm sorry I was the one who told you!" she smiles. "He still loves you though. He just struggles with expressing it around you."

I blush after she says that. *He does, doesn't he,* I think to myself as I let out a small smile of happiness.

Though it quickly dies as I remember that he is leaving. It was nice while it lasted. We all will miss him most definitely.

The area goes quiet as Xena opens the oven, then closes it. Afterward, she looks out of the window cut with broken eyes. Something else is bothering her.

It is kind of hard not to notice that she has a bruise on her neck.

"What is it really, Xena?"

"Nothing. That was all."

I sigh and place my hand on her shoulder. Gently moving her head over to get a better look at her bruise. She allows me to touch her with no care for once.

"Lowell did that, right?"

"Now why would you assume that?"

"Well, it wasn't on you before we left y'all alone. You don't have to cover for her."

"Nothing happened," she says, shoving me off of her.

I notice Richard glance over towards us. I lower my tone to a whisper to not make it seem like were going at it.

"What you two do behind closed doors is all on you. Just be careful," I say motioning at her marks.

She rubs it, taking a quick glance at Lowell. I know those marks are either fight marks or fresh hickeys.

Her face gets cold as she rolls her eyes, "Honestly, I'm tired of y'all telling me to be careful. You act like I can't take care of myself."

She glances out of the window cutout at her. Lowell and Richard are laughing and talking it up. That's a first.

"I'm not angling this to be putting a target on your back. I just told you to be careful one time do not rope me in your outside issues."

She looks at me with a blank stare.

"What are we talking about, Christopher?"

"I'm just saying this is a game of life or death. You can save the freaky sexual stuff for afterwards." I raise an eyebrow. "After all am I wrong in assuming those are either bruises from fighting or hickeys on your neck?"

"Oh," blush spreads over her face. "I didn't realize- I'm sorry, we ran into some conflict while solving a clue."

"Please do not apologize we are well. Enlighten me."

"I touched a mark on her chest, and after a few seconds, her eyes turned completely white. Then she got more, umm…dominant. If that's a word I can use," Xena faintly smiles, looking back at me. Speaking faster.

"And?"

"And it was alarming, Christopher. I don't know, she grabbed my neck softly and kissed the side of it before the other things happened. I told her to stop and started panicking because she was moving too fast, and then she pinned me against the wall. And this creepy ghost creature came out of her back and pushed Lowell's body to the floor. It wrapped its hand over my neck. Then I scratched it and Lowell's body winced. She looked to be dead. I stuck my blade in the ghost person's side as she threatened me, but the creature then started cutting me with her nails.

Whoever it was wasn't going to give Lowell back without a fight. So, I had to fight her until Lowell came back in control and the creature left."

"Oh…wow."

"I'm not crazy. You don't believe me?"

"In a weird way I do, I am just processing what you said."

That made no sense to me but it's probably since she explained it so fast. That does sound completely out of Lowell's character, but it explains why she's so off now. Maybe Richard can explain what happened to Lowell. Nothing like that happened on my golden birthday.

"Yeah. But she didn't remember any of it when she woke up, which is fine."

"So, the marks are-"

"Hickeys, yes, but not because we were purposefully intimate."

The oven beeps, meaning the food is ready. We faintly smile at each other.

My stomach growls quietly.

Taking the food out with oven mitts, Xena grabs two plastic lunch trays to place the tater tots and nuggets on. She then bumps me and smiles as we head to the others with the food.

I sit down across from Lowell, and Xena sits across from Richard. The two trays of food sit in the middle of the four of us. She is next to Lowell and I'm next to Richard.

We all start talking, eating, and grabbing the food once the trays are placed on the table. Granted we all had washed our hands before we started, so there aren't any germs or blood being spread.

As we enjoy each other's company, Xena stands up and starts walking back to the kitchen.

"I'll be back with drinks. I saw sodas in the fridge earlier," she announces.

She skips into the kitchen and we continue talking. I feel like sharks and zombie apocalypses are common topics for tonight's entertainment. Lowell claims that she would beat up the zombies to protect us. And we all concluded that I would be the first person to be bitten.

While we are talking and waiting for Xena to come back, Richard checks the time then clicks his phone off, looking behind him in the direction of where Xena is at. I did not get to see what time it was, but I know he noticed the marks on her neck a little while ago. I can tell he is thinking about something and just doesn't want to ask.

He is always thinking about something. I knew when he joined this game, he knew more than he was leading on.

I remain silent as Xena starts walking back. She drops one of the cans on the floor and picks it up. Placing it on the table and laughing it off, saying that she will take the dropped one. She sits back down next to Lowell.

Lowell is smiling and doing a cute happy dance while munching on her tater tots. Xena is sneakily taking some off and eating them as we run out of food in the middle.

"Can we take a moment to acknowledge everything that happened? I know this is our personal down time but I'm not like you guys, I can't just dismiss it and not think about all the gore and trauma we're going through," Lowell announces breaking the silence.

Richard, Xena, and I exchange looks of uninterest towards acknowledging anything.

"Okay- anything you want birthday girl," I shrug.

"What did you want to say?" Xena asks.

"Oh- I don't know. I just wanted to know I'm not insane in feeling like shit for still living during all of this."

"Well, I died and came back so technically I didn't survive like you three did."

"Yeah, and Christopher and I played before so we're kind of desensitized to all of this- torture," Richard adds.

"Oh okay- I'm sorry from bringing this up," she laughs nervously. "I just- never mind."

"Okay wait- you're right. Living while watching everyone die isn't the easiest," Richard agrees. "Especially when they do not come back or when they do and want nothing to do with you."

"Asking people to play the game is already problematic however if you want a full debrief from this traumatic experience it is best to wait until the game is finished. When we are in a safer place," I explain.

"That sounds good," Lowell smiles.

"Although we do need to talk about all the deaths throughout the game and see if we can predict anything. For either who will die next or if we will make it out," Richard adds.

"Uh…okay. Are we putting them in order or something? Is there a reason?"

"Yes, but I'll explain after," Richard shrugs.

Unzipping his backpack, he pulls out a loose piece of paper and a pencil. Getting ready to write things down. We all just shrug, confused.

"Okay, so Emil was the first to die. At the beginning from an easel. That was around 6 pm or so," Richard writes. Then stops.

"Or maybe it wasn't. I don't remember the time."

"I fail to remember too," I add.

"Same. But Deondra was next. We found her on our way to the clinic with Zoe around 7. D died from bleeding out. I don't know what time. That was maybe around 9 pm since the moon was shining," Lowell adds.

"I think Mark was second though. When we went back to the dorm unit, we found him. He was talking about how she got cut and stuff. That was around 6…6:20, maybe?"

"Yeah, because we finished that first riddle by 5:50," Richard adds to Xena's comment.

"Okay, so none of us know who died second," Lowell says fast.

"Well, no. But while Richard and I were leaving the math classroom, we heard someone say 'don't leave,' if that helps," Xena mentions.

"It does because I heard the same, if not a similar thing. That's what Deondra yelled when we were on our way to the clinic. The sun had already set."

Richard writes Mark's name second and Deondra's third. Putting "by flying knife explosion" and "bleeding out from a deep side cut" next to the corresponding person.

"That makes Zoe fourth?" I ask. We all look at each other. Technically she wasn't dead before we left, and after Lowell came back to life, that's when we checked on her.

"I don't know. We'd have to check her phone and see if she recorded something or when she stopped texting. If it's still alive," I say.

"Mmm, just mark her fourth. She seemed to have died before Xena," Lowell mentions.

Richard then shrugs, marking Zoe fourth. Putting "broken ankle and possible attack."

"I died fifth from drowning," Xena said.

"And me sixth from the same thing."

Richard writes them down too. He puts the paper in the center for all of us to see.

"So, Emil died from an easel then Mark died from knives. They have no relationship, but they were both seen by people. Then Deondra died from bleeding and only one person saw her get cut, while no one saw Zoe get injured or die. It happened behind closed doors," Richard sums up.

"Yes," Lowell and Xena say simultaneously.

"Then Xena and Lowell drowned. Both of them explain that they were attacked underwater. Xena drowned and Lowell was still under the water. Though the water spit Xena out when she was dead. I caught her as Richard was pulling Lowell's body out of the water," I add.

"Yes," the girls say simultaneously again.

Both of them drowned, but Lowell luckily was able to come back on her own. Xena was long gone. Took her longer to come back.

"Putting that all together-" Richard stops mid-sentence.

All three of them then glance at me.

"Y-You're probably next. And it should be in front of us if it cycles back around like that. You'll probably be attacked too but not like the girls or Zoe."

My mouth drops open.

"I'm not dying. Lowell and I got marks from after we died."

"Me too," Richard adds.

"Marked by the creature? What does that even mean?" I question, nervously.

Looking at each of them.

"Well…I died at age 15 during mine. So, I've had this mark for about four years, and honestly, it's been…taking care of me," Richard explains.

"What do you mean?"

"Well, if you let him speak, maybe he'll address your question," Lowell says, nudging me.

I roll my eyes.

"Oh, come on he's just scared," Xena adds nicely. "But yes, save your questions till the end."

Richard smiles for once and looks at me.

"Christopher, I mean that in my experience, you are kind of living through it. The mark is keeping you alive, and because the creature gave it to you, you have a layer of protection. Due to you being able to summon them. Or they can summon you if need be. It's weird. But without the mark, you'd be dead."

"It is weird," I sigh. "And I don't follow?"

"Umm…" he thinks about his next wording. "They kill you, and if they want you then they will mark you. The mark is the creature bringing you back to life. So, the mark is what is keeping me alive to this day."

"Oh."

A light bulb goes off in both girls' heads. Their eyes light up at the same time.

"Wait, you said we can summon them?"

The girls question at the same time. Looking at each other. They smile and start discussing something with each other. Coming to the conclusion that they must have accidentally summoned Lowell's creature which is why Xena got attacked.

"Well, not literally. It's more like if someone tries to kill you or you feel like someone is taking advantage of you, in any way, it affects others that are marked too. But it sends a signal to your creature. The creature will come to kill your biggest threat at the moment. It's almost like a guard."

"Okay, so basically if we get overstimulated with fear the creature will show up?"

"Yes. But you don't have to be scared to summon them. Though if you were, it would have to be from something that's not them. An outside party."

Xena then looks at Lowell. Frowning. She must have scared her in some way.

"Wait, wait you said it doesn't have to be fear? So what else could summon them?" Lowell asks.

"Lust," Richard says bluntly.

"Though that one's more complicated. It just depends on you and which creature marked you."

"Explain," I say.

"Okay, well, for example, say you were marked on the chest, Christopher," he starts.

I nod my head.

"If I touched your mark then you could accidentally summon your creature. If two factors play a role. One, your creature is interested in me, and two-"

"Christopher would have feelings for you too, but be a little scared, causing the creature to investigate why your heart is beating so fast?" Lowell interrupts, finishing his thought.

"Exactly. Feelings of love, interest, lust, et cetera. So it depends on the person and the creature."

I'm guessing that Lowell's creature has some care for Xena along with Lowell liking her too. That's why they surfaced? I'm so confused but telling by everyone else's faces, they understand. It just doesn't make sense to me how a creature aiming to kill you could like you at the same time.

"And how do you know all this? I mean five years is a long time, so you definitely had to find this out the hard way," Xena asks.

Forget these questions, I am still stuck on the fact that I will die next. This means I am going to see this creature face to face, and it could try and kill me.

Or so they say.

Eww. Why would you tell me that?

"I survived a plane crash, met the creature in dozens of nightmares, had to fight him so he didn't kill my ex, and on top of that everyone around me in the real world and game has died. But for me…I'm still here. And marked." Richard shrugs. "If that makes sense. Besides, I took notes every time. Like solving a mystery."

"Well, I didn't stay dead," Xena smiles.

Richard looks at her for a split-second, contemplating life.

"Th-that's right. You didn't," he says looking into space.

Starting to mumble things to himself about why she didn't die. He's surprised. Lowell then clears her throat, causing him to look at her.

"A-and how did you know that your ex at the time was being killed?" Lowell asks, breaking Xena's eye contact.

Xena then looks away and bites her lip.

"Ask me when the game is over, okay?"

"Okay."

It grows silent. Xena opens her mouth to say something but then takes a drink of her soda. Looking at me. I shrug and raise an eyebrow. Indicating for her to say something about what she told me.

"So, say that you- I- a person finds, no, summons the creature while you and someone else are just touching each other's marks and the person does- have possible but not proven feelings for you. Would it be possible that the creature would ki- mm," Xena says nervously struggling to find the wording.

"Never mind."

Lowell looks at her, confused, as Richard smiles. He places his hand on hers before looking down at his food. Moving his hand, he looks over at Lowell.

"Fine. If you want, I can talk about one of my fearful love-lust summonings," he suggests.

Lowell's eyes widen.

"You're going to talk about your ex?" She says happily.

I raise an eyebrow kinda excited too but focusing on the fact that he said "one of." Richard is a closed-off person. It almost feels illegal to be in a conversation like this with him. Like I must pay for this free conversation.

"Yes. It may help answer some of your questions," he glances at Xena.

She then glances at Lowell. Lowell avoids looking at her, but her face slightly turns red.

"I'll keep it short. This was my first time summoning my creature. As awkward as it was, we were getting into something sexual which made it worse. We were just making out and somewhere down the line, my ex placed their hand on my chest. Just to rest it there as they sat on top of me. I was nervous, yes, it was my first time doing anything sexual in this case…" he pauses.

I smile slightly, as all of us look highly interested. Our chins rest on our hands as we all maintain eye contact with him. Like kids in a huddle while the teacher reads a book in their rocking chair. He looks slightly hurt to be telling this story.

"Umm…out of nowhere everything went black for me. I was in a huge, dark, empty space. I failed to see anything, but I could hear a few sounds coming from my partner."

"What kind of sounds?" Lowell asks but for once not in a joking way.

She asks it in a way that is more of her trying to relate than make this awkward.

"Not sexual sounds, if that's what you're thinking. More like screaming or crying for help because you're about to die. These painful sounds were heard around me as I randomly felt scratching on my back and arms. I was scared but couldn't do anything about it. When I was awakened, I had no recollection of what happened. The only thing I saw was the bloody body of my ex laying on my bed. Lifeless. A burn mark lay on the head of the bed frame that wasn't there before," he frowns, looking at the exit door.

Away from us.

"Moral of the story, my creature killed them. And I played a part in it because I decided to have feelings for someone. Not knowing what having this mark meant. You could argue that I wasn't in control and that's true but it was still my body that was being used by my creature to hurt them. And that's my fault. So, for a love-lust summoning to happen the feelings wouldn't be platonic. And honestly you don't have to even be in a relationship or close with the person. I've lost a friend too."

Xena looks at Lowell. Lowell glances into her eyes and looks away, upset. I look over at Richard, rubbing his back. He looks back at me.

"But don't worry. If both of y'all were marked, it may go differently. As in, if my ex was marked."

"I get it. Your ex died, but earlier you said that this was 'one' of your lust incidents. Is there another one where you saved a different ex?" I ask.

"Guys, stop with the questions, he's already said what he needed to say," Xena defends.

Richard looks at her smiling, then back at me, nodding his head in agreement with her.

"It's just a simple question, it's not like we are prying," Lowell argues back.

"You are prying though. It's personal."

"I know, but it's for educational purposes. We all know Richard came into the game knowing more than he led on, so let him talk about it."

"If we do that, we'll never finish the game, and this conversation will lead us to our deaths," Xena adds, slightly angered. "Besides, what's the point in knowing more if we can do this when the game ends, Lowell?"

"Because I want to know what the hell happened in that bathroom," she snaps, standing up. She proceeds to walk away, but Xena grabs her hand.

Xena rolls her eyes.

"Please stay."

Lowell's eyes water.

"Nothing happened. We can move on from that," Xena says softly, trying not to escalate the situation.

Richard and I glance at each other. Remaining quiet.

"We can't when you were the one about to be killed."

"But I'm still here."

"I know, but you almost weren't."

"Shit, neither were you. I had to do that heavy lifting and take all that stuff while you stayed in your pitch-black room listening, I guess."

"Xena don't paint it like the darkness is easy," Richard says.

I nudge him, slightly laughing.

"Sounds like the easier part. Xena was fighting for her life after all."

"Exactly," Xena agrees.

Richard rolls his eyes.

"Yes, but I wasn't aiming to push you into that situation. It just happened," Lowell rolls her eyes. "I blame myself but at least you made me feel okay about it. Like it wasn't my fault but now…I'm scared. We said we would find out what was going on and now that Richard is saying everything, you don't want to hear it."

Xena sighs and looks Lowell in the eyes.

"I know. I want to talk privately though, not everyone needs to know everything. Because the only thing that ran through my mind during that whole situation was not 'let me get to safety,' it was 'I need to get Lowell out of here.' I don't care about my life as I do yours right now."

"Because it's my birthday," Lowell sighs, angered.

Pointing at us two boys now and then Xena.

"The only reason why any of you three care about me surviving is that if I die, you die too."

"Well duh, at this point in the game, yes," Richard mumbles.

I nudge him, telling him to shut up.

Even though I agree with him. I hate to think like this but at this point in the game, I do care about my life, so I want her to survive so I don't die. If that makes me a terrible friend, then so be it. But she's in control of all our lives right now solely by existing. That's the reality she must face.

Lowell looks at him meanly and he looks back at her like "What? I said what I said."

Lowell looks upset and just rolls her eyes. Xena frowns.

"I'm not gonna lie to you, Lowell, you need to face the fact that your mere existence tonight impacts our lives. You control it," Richard adds sharply.

Not soothingly like how he normally speaks.

"No hard feelings, but we joined knowing that we were okay with putting your life before ours. That does not mean we want to die though," I add.

"Besides, if we die and don't come back, it's traumatic. The blame goes to you," Richard adds.

"And if we separate at the end of this, then it's still all on you.

Not us. You."

Lowell frowns, sitting back down. Xena presses her hand on her shoulders and rolls her eyes.

"Well, listen you don't have to believe me, but I joined knowing nothing about this. I joined just like the rest of us…to help you."

She then takes a large sip of the rest of her soda.

"Besides. I am surprised I lived to see my college years. Might as well die the way I want," she sighs, getting up.

Leaving to go to the kitchen with her empty can.

It grows quiet.

"I would love to answer the rest of your questions later. But honestly, she is right, Lowell," Richard sighs, rolling his eyes.

"Xena... "

He then pauses and looks at me.

Lowell looks into the kitchen. The sound of the fridge door closing can be heard.

I place my hand on her shoulder across the table.

"She wouldn't willingly take a bullet for you. But she knows you deserve someone who gives a fuck about you. Not the fake love you are used to," I add, as Xena walks over to us with nothing in her hand.

"You need to stop thinking that all girls are out to get you."

"Why does she care?"

"I don't know," Richard sighs in a soft voice. "She's just like that. She shows people what she needs by being to us what she needs."

Xena sits back down next to Lowell, not looking at her. Lowell frowns.

The clock on the wall then clicks loudly, and we look over at it.

Two and a half hours left of the game.

"Can we just talk about all this later if we make it out of here? Besides, if you guys are already marked and have gone through this already, then that means their plan is in motion," he smiles. "It could explain what he told me the first time he ever marked me," Richard mumbles.

"What'd he say?"

"He said-"

…

“So he needs-”

…

“What if we just-”

"Christopher, are you okay?" Richard says, worriedly waving his hand in front of my face.

"What?"

"You spaced out after we told you you might die next and after Richard's storytime," Lowell frowns.

"Oh."

"So that "marking" conversation we had didn't happen?" I say.

I don't know anything about marks or what this is so I couldn't have created the conversation on my own, could I?

"Oh, no, it did. You just slowly spaced out and stopped responding," Richard says, placing a hand on my head to measure the heat.

His hands are cold, but my head is hot.

Xena stands up and walks over to the door. Throwing her trash in the can before looking at us.

"Come on," she waves. "This game won't finish itself.”

Blood Stains {Christopher's Mark}

This kid Christopher gets terrified easily. So I cover my hand over his eyes as he lays still against the wall. Such a beautiful man, I must say. Perfect switch. As I continue to cover his eyes, he lays asleep with his back against the wall. My other hand finds its way to his chest. Less pain if I mark him before he wakes up. Letting out a deep breath, I touch his chest with my finger and wait 20 seconds until it's completed. If not a full 20 seconds, there's a chance of other creatures finding our markings and killing them in their world.

Moving my hand off his eyes, I glance at his head. It's cracked. Scared, I stand up and pace around.

"My boy isn't breathing!" I yell as if someone else will show up.

Shaking my hands nervously, I crouch back down. Placing my hand over the crack. Closing my eyes, I attempt to heal his wound. This will be my first time doing this ritual. I knew I should have reviewed my notes on spells before this birthday. Z and K are going to kill me if this kid dies.

"What are you doing, Frilo?" Pandora says from behind me.

"Trying to save my human," I reply nervously.

"Just blow the smoke over him. He's not dead yet, relax," she says, rolling her eyes.

Pointing at his chest rising and falling. She starts walking away. I forgot what breathing looks like.

"Please don't tell the others," I say, blowing the smoke over him.

The crack heals over.

"I won't have to. Seems like you're not the only one making mistakes tonight."

"What do you mean?"

"We have a meeting to attend in a few moments. Dress presentable, love."

Five Marks? {Richard}

Christopher was holding the door open for us as we walked out of the library. The lights flickered and the next thing we knew, he was holding his head before passing out on the ground. I rush over to him as a creature touches his chest. Making deadly eye contact with me, causing me to stop a foot in front of him. He then looks away and I rock Christopher softly by his arms and close the door. To see if he'll wake.

I don't recognize the creature that touched him. This creature had a cloak on, and ridiculously long nails and legs. 1) I thought it was only those two siblings and 2) I've never seen a creature in person other than the one with spikes. This one looks more like a masculine-presenting 11-foot ghost-succubus hybrid. With no wings.

Christopher slowly leans against the wall holding his chest.

Eyes closed.

"Are you okay?" I ask, while thinking to myself, *Are you marked?,* but knowing that that was probably going to be something I'd have to see on him later.

I assume that he is, due to the conversation we had, but he was the most confused in our conversation and that wasn't hard to see.

He gasps for air, looking around scared.

We all look at each other.

"Umm…my heart had stopped."

"Welp, that's a sign that we need to just finish this game," Lowell yells from behind us, holding a note.

"Where did you get that?"

"I found it back in the swimming center. I forgot about it until I had dug into my pockets a few seconds ago."

We all glance at each other nervously. To me, getting cards will never be the scariest thing in this game. I find it enjoyable.

She passes the note around as we read it in our heads. It reads:

Five I need
Marked by me
Jump through the fire
But don't leave

And if you're alive
When it dies
Then the game is complete
So you will sleep

"Five?" Xena says in a confused tone. We all look at each other, knowing that there are only four of us. Shrugging it off after replying with "It shouldn't affect the game," I look at my phone to see what time it is. It is 3 o'clock on the dot.

How could that be? Time is going by too fast; I honestly thought we were in the cafeteria for an hour.

Just as I look up at the others to mention our time limit, the fire alarm rings loudly in the distance. The only issue is that there is no fire in sight.

"Let's go back to the library. Remember that the previous note said the prize was in there, so maybe a fire broke out there."

"Okay, but we have to stay close to the ground and to each other."

Just before we head back up the stairs, we see a door fall over the rail from the floor above us.

Curious, but not too curious, I run out onto the yard and look up to see where it came from.

The fire is blazing through the second floor. And by the looks of the door laying on the grass in front of me, it's from the library.

I look at the others as they are standing in a circle with their hands on top of each other.

They stare at me, waiting for me to put my hand on top as if we are doing a team hand stack. Once I place mine on top, a strong emotional connection to everyone else forms in my heart. I've never felt this way before. It is like I have been with these three my whole life and nothing could change that. Or in the words of Xena: "I think we just spiritually connected our souls."

Looking at my aggressively tingling hands, a purple color lights up my veins. Looking around, it does the same with everyone else, making all of us quickly pull our hands away from each other. Once our hearts settle and we are no longer touching, the color leaves. And so does most of my fear. *It seems like all the fear inside of me was shared among us,* I think before shaking my head "no," because that makes no sense. All my creature told me four years ago was, "*You are the first to be marked, but there will be a group of you all. You won't see it coming, but they will need you*" in sign language.

It took me months to decipher the individual hand gestures because I don't know ASL, so I could still be wrong.

Silence spreads as we slowly turn our heads at the blazing buildings. Even the stars in the sky and the red tree a few feet behind us can't make this moment any less intimidating.

A loud sigh then comes from Lowell, breaking the silence.

"Umm, so are we finishing today or what?" Lowell says, walking with her back towards the fire.

Christopher shouts "Race you there!" and sprints towards the building and up the stairs.

The rest of us start running after him. He is fast.

When we get to the second floor we crouch along the wall, Christopher in the front, followed by Lowell, Xena, and then me. Once at the front of the door, we stop walking. Peeking inside, Christopher and Lowell move to the other side of the door while Xena and I crouch on the floor, still. Nervous, Christopher nods his head. Christopher and Lowell then go to the left so Xena and I head to the right.

We start to crawl across the heated carpet floor while the fire blazes around us. The bookshelves and books are scattered everywhere, but there isn't as much fire in the library compared to the hallway. It mostly looks like a tornado ran through the place.

In the distance, a tall ring of fire at the back of the library is noticeable. On top of that, there is no smoke rising to the ceiling in that one area.

Tapping Xena on the back, I point at the fire ring. The best way to get to the back of the library without getting hurt by falling bookshelves would be to crawl against the side walls.

I want to ask her why she didn't think she would see her college years, but now might not be a good time.

As we continue crawling, it starts becoming ridiculously hard to breathe, so I cover my nose with the top of my shirt. The shards of glass and broken wood cutting into my skin with every step. I can barely see with all the fire and smoke in the air. All I know is that the view of Xena's butt is getting farther and farther away. I'm not the only one getting tired of this crawling. Xena stops in front of me and leans against the wall, trying to breathe. Her face is red, and her clothes are torn at the legs.

"Why did you stop?" I ask worriedly.

"You're falling behind. We are almost to the fire ring so it's best if I follow you so I can make sure I don't lose you to this heat," she replies, motioning me forward.

Nodding my head, I climb over her legs and continue to crawl against the wall. She follows close behind me as we get closer and closer to the fire ring. Books continue to fall around us, as the cuts and burns on my hands bleed worse. Pain shooting through them.

As painful as it was to crawl, we finally made it close to the fire ring. Through the fallen bookshelves I see a small gap open that we can crawl through without getting ourselves killed. It is high so we would have to stand up and climb on top of the bookshelf.

Going through one of the only open holes. Whispering to Xena the plan, she quickly pulls her leg in as a hot metal rod falls next to her. It lays against her skin as she moans in pain.

Scared and in pain, her breathing starts to speed up, so I place my hand on the pole next to hers as we move it off. Reassuring her that I'm still here. We nod at each other as I stand up and pull myself in between one of the fallen shelves.

Just as I am able to pull my leg through, another bookshelf falls on top, causing the whole thing to catch on fire. Leaving no safe passage or opening for Xena.

Trapping her on the other side.

"Are you okay?" I yell.

"Yeah, just go on without me. I'll find another way through," she yells back.

"Okay, but if you face any trouble then just yell for me or the others. Even with the loud crashes going on, I will still come out to find you."

"Richard, I will be fine. If I don't come back in time, then just finish the game okay?" she reassures.

"Wait!"

It goes silent.

"Xena!" I yell.

No response. She doesn't want me to save her.

Sometimes it's like she doesn't like being around me. She makes so many excuses and chooses people other than me. We used to be so much closer.

I sigh, brushing off those thoughts.

Fuck this game! I think to myself as I quickly run over and look for a way to get inside of the firewall. Like I saw earlier, there is no fire on the inside, so I know for a fact that once inside we will be safe. At least I'm 90% sure it's safe. That's where the prize should be at.

Looking around, I see a huge, steel, square-type ring, so I place it into a part of the firewall. Watching as the fire in the area moves around it, leaving a small slit that I can squeeze inside of.

"Oh, thank goodness," I sigh once inside.

Sitting on the ground, I place my hand in my head and let out my bottled-up tears. On the bright side, the temperature in this firewall is surprisingly cool, but if I lose Xena again… I wouldn't know what to do.

Center Of The Fire {Lowell}

"We should probably take a break…from talking…because the more we talk…the more toxins we breathe in," Christopher yawns as we climb through the bookcase.

This smoke is filling up my lungs. I'm surprised we're not dead yet.

"Okay, but that means that we are going…to have to move faster…and stay closer," I add in, taking quick breaths.

"Alright."

It is like a maze of fallen bookshelves and fire that we are crawling through.

I don't regret letting Christopher convince me to crawl through the middle of the library to find the prize. The only issue is that we don't know where we are going or what we are looking for.

We are just quickly moving and sliding through the bookshelves. In the distance, my ear catches the sounds of Richard and Xena yelling. I figure that either they have run into some trouble or they are fighting.

I couldn't make out their words completely, but they seem to have broken up.

Christopher and I continue, sliding our flexible bodies through the bookshelves until we reach a small open space under a table that is on fire. We crawl closer to the ground, chest now dragging across it, as we make our way under. Trying not to catch on fire.

Once we safely get through we stand up, covering our mouths and climb over another bookshelf that had fallen on its side. This whole time our pattern of moving has been crawl, crouch, stand, crawl through something, drop to the ground. Then repeat.

Until now I never realized how many bookshelves our school library has. Though I kind of like parkour. It just would have been more fun crawling and jumping over them if they weren't on fire.

I got burned twice.

"You never answered my question before," he says while I help him climb down another bookshelf.

"It doesn't matter, she already knows I have some sort of interest for her."

"'Cause you are falling in love with her," he says in disbelief. We continue crawling on the ground again.

"No, our chemistry isn't that tight. That's a big word."

Am I falling in love? I hope not, but she does already know I have feelings or an interest. She probably doesn't feel the same. She's just nice.

He then mumbles something to himself that contradicts what I just said, but I struggle to hear his exact words.

"But I don't know. She just being nice honestly."

He smiles and says, "Go for it. She seems to be alright, honestly."

In comparison to me, Christopher does have different values in a relationship. It's weird to hear him say this though.

"Well, we tease each other, yes, but getting to know her - I'm just terrified, Christopher. I want someone who's soul is so intertwined with mine that the thought of her loving me will break my heart. Yet give me pure love and joy at the same time. That's probably why my creature showed up," I explain.

"You want that with her?"

"I don't know."

It goes quiet for a few moments.

My fear of losing Xena is strong for only knowing her for a short period. Just as strong as my will to be with her romantically. Which is something I'll have to work on, because I'm tired of running from my fears.

Though if it wasn't for this game, none of us would be hanging out, so I'm happy we're all here. I guess in the end it'll be hard to hurt each other. We've been through too many emotions and pain for one night.

"Would me liking her change our dynamic? You know… because of last night."

"I enjoyed last night but we are always drunk when we get intimate. It is never serious nor is it public information. We do not have to stop."

I nod.

Covering my nose with my shirt, we continue crawling. Faster now since we were crawling slower while we talked.

After a while of crawling forward towards the back of the library, we see a huge fire circle. Poking Christopher to get his attention, I point at the fire circle so we can head there. It crossed my mind that Richard and Xena probably saw that first and decided to head there. They are both smart like that.

Yawning, I look back at Christopher who is crawling behind me. His hands are free from blood.

Getting tired of crawling with bloody hands and cuts on my face from the books that have hit me. Christopher comes next to me as I crawl through the last bookshelf that is in front of the fire circle. I turn around again to see if Christopher is crawling through when Xena jumps through an opening of the bookshelf to the right of me. Another one falls right after. A loud crash comes from the area she jumped through. She lands on me.

The bookshelf catches fire as a wood plank sticks through in her leg. The rest of her body is on top of mine because she fell on me. Her heart races faster while she pulls to free herself.

I watch a huge cut start forming on the side of her calf muscle. Blood viciously pours out as tears run down her face.

She isn't screaming but she is biting her lip and digging her stubby nails into my leg while trying to pull her foot out. Wincing in pain, I help her pull her foot out of the shelf as quickly as possible.

I end up pulling her so hard that we crash into Christopher behind us.

She lets out a scream.

In a quick motion, his back slams against the bookshelf, causing his arm to drag against a broken piece of wood. He seems unbothered as we glance at him. He then yells "Watch out!" and moves to the side.

A small, sharp, metal pole from the ceiling falls and goes straight through my left thigh. It's hollow.

"Ahhh!!" I scream in agonizing pain. Freaking out as blood pours down.

Tears running down my face as I lay on the floor. Having no choice but to let the blood and pus flow out of my leg. Then a book falls and hits my head. A huge dictionary, to be more specific.

Christopher's eyes lock onto the metal pole in my leg. Other than the ringing in my ears, I can hear him throwing up in the corner. I just bite my lip and clench one of my fists as I try to turn over with the other arm. Xena crouches over me, snapping her fingers to keep me focused on her. Ripping off a long piece of her already torn shirt, tightening it on top of my thigh over the wound.

She then tries to stand up and come over to help Christopher as he throws up.

Instead of wasting any more time, Christopher walks out first as Xena helps me hobble on my other leg. My arm over her shoulder.

Leaving a blood trail behind us as we all crawl through an opening in the fire circle.

"Wow, you guys look like you were in a fight," Richard laughs, trying to make light of the situation. It's easy to see that he was crying prior to our arrival. His eyes are puffy.

"Nah, the pole is a new accessory I was eyeing and finally had a chance to try on," I reply sarcastically. Wincing.

"My bad," Xena says, in response to my sarcasm.

It hurts to laugh, but the four of us start laughing at our pain anyway. I wince again. "All's fine," I say to her.

The fire circle that we are in is an oxygen pocket. And it's cooler than it is outside this ring.

Looking around, I notice that there is a stand in the middle of the circle. On top of the stand is a necklace with the number three on it and a slot in the center.

When I limp over to the stand and reach for the necklace, I am thrown backward. Luckily Christopher grabs me instead of the fire catching me. He and I both let out a slight moan as I look down and realize he caught me with his cut arm. Even though he wrapped it with Richard's scarf a few seconds ago.

I quickly get off of him with the help of Xena, and thank him for saving me.

"We need a plan," Richard says, looking at the blood on my leg.

His face turns green like he wants to throw up also.

"Do y'all have any ideas of how I should grab it?" I ask. Silence.

"I don't know. I got a ring with the number two on it when I finished my game at 15. But I didn't have to work to retrieve it," Richard says.

"Same. I got an anklet with the number one on it when I finished mine. I didn't do anything to retrieve it either, it just showed up," Christopher adds in.

Xena yawns. Inspecting the slot. She shrugs and drops in a card she has in her pocket. A light on the inside glows green.

"Just drop your cards in here and then you should be able to grab it. I don't know how many, so just put in all the ones you have."

"Alrighty," Christopher optimistically replies, smiling.

"And if we die, we die as a group."

He then drops the one in and Richard laughs before dropping in his few. I hand mine to Xena and she drops in the rest. We drop in all of them. Feeling like it's too easy.

Either way, two loud beeps ring through the air. It takes a few seconds of us just standing there, but the fire slowly starts to go down until it completely disappears.

Excitement spreads over us as we all start hugging and laughing because we completed the game. Halfway through our cheers, my head starts pounding. Light-headed from the blood loss. My vision soon gets blurry too.

All I can hear is Richard asking me if I'm okay, and Xena asking if Christopher is okay.

The last thing I felt was my body fall to the floor. My eyes close completely.

The once hard floor feels soft now.

The Bridge Between

• • •

Investigating {Xena}

I jolt up out of my bed, my clothes drenched in sweat. Coagulated blood scratches on my feet. It's still painful to walk. My head is throbbing and everything feels like a nightmare. Slowly coming back to me.

But for once I feel more like myself.

Looking around the room, I see Deondra lying peacefully in her bed. She looks perfectly fine. No scars, no blood. Looking away, I softly press my hand on the side of my bed. A voice inside tells me to *Look at your hand* but when I do, there is nothing there. No scars, no cuts, no blood.

I'm confused.

One thing leads to another, I hear screaming come from someone's room. It startles both me and Deondra. We run out of our room and see Emil, Richard, and Christopher standing in front of Zoe's room.

I peek my head inside the door, hoping that Lowell wasn't beating her up. Luckily it is the total opposite. From what I can see, Zoe is provoking Lowell and Lowell looks like she is about to curse her out. So the scream was probably due to yelling back and forth. Not a physical fight.

"Zoe, sweetheart, please leave Lowell alone," Emil says.

"You two get into too many fights and may end up killing each other. I suggest that y'all get new dorm buddies because you darlings clearly don't like each other," Deondra soothes.

"Please! Please! I will take anyone else at this point," Zoe begs, sticking her tongue out at Lowell.

"Fucking childish you are," Lowell says.

"Well, I am better friends with you than I am with Xena so I can be your roommate and Xena can be Lowell's. If that's okay with you, Xena. Hopefully, you don't see this as me trading you up because I do adore you as my roommate."

"Of course I don't see it like that, you know how it is," I laugh, rolling my eyes at Zoe and Lowell.

I wonder if Lowell realizes that her pants have a huge cut in the front where that pole was last night. Zoe, Emil, and Mark look fine though. No scars or anything.

"Yes," Deondra smiles.

After settling the situation between these two, I start moving into Lowell's dorm and Zoe moves into my old one with Deondra. It took about 2 hours to move my stuff, but happiness fills me as it is finally over.

I plop on the couch.

On the verge of being completely asleep, a buzz comes from my phone. An email notification appears on my lock screen while I lay down on the couch. Too tired to open it, I just let myself drift off to sleep.

Though I couldn't have been knocked out nearly long enough after that. When I wake up again, my phone is missing and a woman's screaming.

Can people stop screaming, please? It's bothering my ears.

Richard runs over to me, dragging me off the couch and over to his and Christopher's room. Didn't even give me time to stand up. I continue laying on the floor, rolling over on my stomach. Their room is very spacious, but you can see the differences in their personalities.

Christopher's side is full of theatrical posters and dance medals, while Richard's is full of poetry books and African American TV show posters. We share a similar taste in posters.

"What's going on? Is someone hurt?" I ask worriedly.

Rubbing my eyes.

"Check your email," Christopher says, jumping up and down with happiness.

"Okay, okay," I laugh.

Pulling out my phone, I click on the email notification I ignored earlier. It is from our manager. I figure that my plan had worked. Smiling while scrolling through it, it says that my pay was raised by ten dollars. So now I make 20 dollars an hour and not 10.

"Wow, this is amazing. I knew my threatening skills were good but not this good," I laugh.

"I know, right," Christopher beams. "But like I didn't really know, I am just so happy."

I watch as Lowell continues to scroll through her phone. It looks as if she has found some more amazing news about her job. After reading it she stares at me, speechless.

The room goes quiet as all their eyes are on me.

"You did this, didn't you?" she smiles.

"Are you referring to the pay raise or the fact that you are the new DJ at the club?" I grin.

"Wait, what?" Christopher's eyes grow wide along with his smile. "You finally get to be our DJ. Lowell, that is amazing!"

"I'm happy for you. We should celebrate tonight before you switch positions," Richard adds.

Richard used to work as a bouncer at the club, but now he works with our local publishing company across the street as an editor. He knows so much about the club because of his past work experience, which is why he understands how important this is for Lowell. I think they also worked at the same time at one point but only for a month, so they never got to know each other.

"How did you convince him? I thought he wouldn't let girls DJ," she asks in amazement.

"Through deep blackmail," I shrug, putting a finger to my lip. "He didn't want to lose his business, so I told him I wanted every employee to have a pay raise and for Lowell to be our new DJ. Also, I made a new rule that his employees can work whatever position they meet qualifications for so if you don't want to be a runner then you can make him change it. So yeah, that was about it," I shrug.

"Wow, blackmail, huh? This is the only place that we are allowed to work, and I've been there for three years soaking up his negative actions. Thank you so much for being the change!" Christopher marvels.

"It's not that serious, I just wanted to do something nice for y'all. It was nothing. Besides, what do you mean that's the only place we can work? We are adults, 18 and older, we're allowed anywhere here," I roll my eyes, smiling.

"Our town is homophobic. That's the only area we can work without being hate-crimed for the most part," Richard says, rubbing my head. "The company protects 100% of the workers that are Queer in some way and doesn't deduct our pay or benefits for it. But still get treated like shit while working either way."

"How do you know?"

"This town is small. Word spreads quickly once you either come out or are outed. There's no reason to lie about your sexuality just to work at a queer club, but there are two allies that work here," Lowell adds.

For the next five minutes, the three of us - Richard, Christopher, and I - continue to talk about work and everyday life. Lowell sits on her bed staring at her phone in silence.

I glance at her, wondering what she is thinking about. Maybe I didn't do the right thing, but in a way, I think she's just shocked.

As I think about her, I don't realize that I'm staring at her so deeply. Our eyes then meet. I quickly dart my gaze from her.

The room slowly grows louder as Lowell says out of nowhere, "Have you ever considered being with a girl?"

The boys go mute. Silence filling the room awkwardly.

Bold question, I think to myself. Even to my standards.

I avoid her eye contact.

I try thinking of what to say but no words are coming out. It is like I am scared to answer, but more scared to hear her response and figure out why she asked that. Just as I gather my words to be able to answer, we hear a female scream coming from the lounge area. Jumping out of my skin, the four of us run out of the bedroom.

Personally, checking out where screaming is coming from is something I would have never done before Lowell's birthday game. It scares me that I actually do it now.

"Is everyone okay?" Christopher asks from the kitchen.

Emil is sitting on the couch rocking back and forth like he had seen a ghost. I can see the fear in his eyes.

My heart races as I stare at him. My hand quickly flies to my mouth as I see a huge gaping hole in his chest. Blood running down into the floor around him. I shut my eyes hard, but once I open them, he is no longer hurt. Lowell places her hand on my shoulders to comfort me.

I think to myself, *I must be seeing things.*

"Everything is okay. Emil just walked by the easel and freaked out. He claims that the easel is after him but, to be honest, he is just going crazy," Mark laughs.

"Honestly darling, you can't scare yourself like that. You should just go outside and calm yourself down by taking photos," Deondra adds.

"Maybe you're right, but I swear it felt like the easel was ready to kill me," Emil's voice shook, as he randomly starts coughing dramatically. "Right through my stomach."

"Yeah, okay love. Let's go get some fresh air and we can move the easel later," Zoe giggles.

"I guess they don't remember what happened yesterday," I whisper to Richard.

"Exactly, but I'm with Emil. To some extent, I do feel the twins' presence here," he nervously laughs.

"Me too, but maybe it has something to do with our marks. Besides we never released him like our note said to do," I whisper, shrugging. "Also, do you see blood on Lowell or me? Because your hand was bloody earlier and same with Christopher."

"No, I don't. You have no wounds in my eyes and neither does Christopher or me."

I look down. I no longer have the scratches, blood, or sweat I saw earlier. I'm so confused about what's happening.

We pause talking as Zoe grabs Emil's arm, guiding him out of the dorm. The four of us then walk back into Lowell's and my room, closing the door behind us. Richard and Christopher jump onto my bed, immediately engaging in conversation and taking up all the space. So I walk over to the closet, making a small passionate glance at her.

It is silent between us.

HOLLOW REALM: BEFORE THE SUMMONING

The dark room screams death around them. Little red skull lights hang from the corner as five chairs surround a table in the center of the room. That table has a single dark book in the center. Nothing else filling the huge empty room.

Three of them walk in, Mara sits patiently. Waiting for the others to sit.

His sister, Zilla, sits down to the right of him. Frilo sits down to the left of him. Pandora sits next to her as she gives her a passionate glance. That glance is not able to be shared anymore.

"*You called us*?" Pandora says along with signing, to break the silence.

Sign language is the only way to communicate with Mara. Though speaking is the only way to communicate with Zilla. Z is blind, Mara is deaf, the other two, Pandora and Frilo, have all six senses for communication. As for the fifth member, Ubel, he's mute. Yet he's always either a no-show or late. He doesn't stay long.

Everyone else talks aloud and signs.

"*Yes*," Z replies. "*I messed up my marking and failed to complete it. She fought me.*"

"*Sounds like prime choice then*," Frilo jokes along with signing. "*I'm serious though.*"

"*I know, but I don't see the issue. We just have to hope for the best, right*?"

"Of course you can't see the issue. Your eyes no longer function," Frilo adds.

Zilla hits him with perfect aim, and he smiles.

"*No*," Pandora adds, sighing. "*If we don't kill them, then someone else will. And with the marks we placed on them, they will only grow stronger as a team.*"

"*That's the point. Mark them and go on about our days*," Frilo adds.

Pandora whispers, "*Where the hell did we get this kid,*" causing Zilla to laugh.

"*Settle down,*" Mara snaps, breaking the noise.

Frilo's heart beats faster. And Pandora glances over at him. She stares at it for a long time before glancing away. Sadness across her face.

"*Listen comrades, and listen carefully. We will not mess up this plan. The only thing we can do is try to get them to come back. By all means necessary.*"

"*Dead or alive?*" Ubel signs, entering through the secret roof latch on the ceiling.

They drop to the ground softly. Making no noise.

"*Look who finally showed up,*" Frilo mumbles, nudging Z.

Z holds her hand out as Ubel grabs it softly. They sign to us with the other hand as Pandora also says aloud what Ubel is saying. Frilo is learning ASL, so he's still rusty with everything they do. That's what he gets for joining and then leaving weeks later in our past lives.

"*Ubel said that they found a new human.*"

"*Who's they?*" Frilo asks.

We all look at him, laughing.

"*Ubel is they.*"

Everyone then nods simultaneously.

"*Dead or alive?*" Ubel signs again.

Smiling at Frilo.

"*Alive, preferably. But perhaps if you bring yours back dead, it's acceptable…I want mine alive, though,*" Mara signs with a grin.

He slowly gets up. Exiting out the door behind his chair. His door. It's one of five doors in this room, leading to who knows what. He doesn't open it for anyone to see his chambers.

"*You heard my brother. Bring them back before the others steal our kill,*" Z announces softly, standing up.

Pulling her cloak hood over her curly, 7-foot long hair.

"*Okay, but why are we even wasting time on these four…*"

"*Five,*" Ubel interrupts.

"*Yes, five. Why are we wasting time on them? Just last week we killed enough to make a city.*"

"*Because we are trying to be freed. Or so K says,*" Pandora replies in a raspy tone.

"*I still don't understand,*" Frilo rebukes. "*This is our life now. Why do we need to be freed?*"

"*Because we just need to be okay. Stop trying to find a meaning to everything and just trust K on this. Maybe he has a good plan,*" Pandora says, turning around sharply. "*And this is not life. This is death.*"

Her silk dress flows around her body for a split second until she fully disappears into thin air. Ubel is also nowhere to be seen, and the roof latch is now closed. With only Frilo and Zilla left in the room, he stands up. Z takes closer steps to her door so she can leave. She holds her hand out in front of her while using her other senses to guide her.

"*Wait!*" He begs. Her back turned to him. "*Can't you promise me that you'll at least try not to kill your human?*"

"*I can't make those types of promises…*" she pauses. "*But maybe she'll kill herself. After all, I didn't completely mark her. Unless I do soon, she'll slowly lose her mind more than she already has.*"

She smiles wickedly and walks off. Closing the door behind her as Frilo stands there watching. Glancing at the roof latch for a moment, saying aloud to himself, "*I'm sorry I failed to be there for you,*" as he walks through his door.

Not knowing that Ubel was sitting in the vent listening to every word of what he said. He then crawls away.

Frilo's the youngest member of the group and for some reason, he feels the need to save his humans. He's had 7 already. More than the others, because he keeps killing them by accident.

Though unlike the others, his heart hasn't left his unliving body yet.

That's why they call him the newbie.

They all have a purpose and he's just learning his.

Richard was private investigating and found out where Kindal and Ziona lived in their early years. Even though the house is currently burned down, the remains were mostly untouched because rumor has it, the land wouldn't allow anyone to take anything from the scene.

He tells the group since it's only a 15-minute walk. However, he wants to give them the space to make that decision to investigate because of yesterday's intensities. He's the type to keep pushing and learning things, it keeps him distracted, but he understands the rest of the group might be tired or uninterested.

Christopher and Richard change into something more relaxing before all four of us leave the dorm unit. The girls say we have a tendency to overdress everywhere but we see it as casual. Through some no so heavy convincing, they agreed to go since it allows them to get away from the dorms for a while and clear their heads.

Locking the dorm door, they skate through the hallways as people jump out of the way. The hallways are noisy and the lights are working today. Taking the elevator down to the main floor. Richard looks at the address once again while they ride the elevator. Realizing that this isn't in a neighborhood, he just keeps quiet about it. It doesn't matter completely.

Once they get off campus, they see little to no cars on the road. Autumn trees line the sides of the road as pedestrians' jog along the sidewalks. The blue sky is beautifully colored as the wind sings in our ears.

They skated on the right side of the street, turning down 'Crystal View Road' and making a right into the 'Desert Prairie'. Desert prairie is an area of the town that was deserted years ago because people reported sightings of demonic activity.

They slowly skate down the gravel road, standing close to each other. The sudden change from beautiful blue skies to gray gives me the chills, but everything is fine. Lowell and Xena are skating hand in hand with each other, and Christopher is looking around admiring the scenery. Dead grass covers empty lawns along with posts that have fallen on stretches along the road, giving this place a voidish character. Along with that, smog fills the air, making it hard to breathe.

Richard leads the others to a roundabout at the end of the neighborhood where the burned down house is located. Surprisingly, there is a single house next to the remains that is still standing, but it looks depressing.

They stop skating and look at the remains.

There is caution tape around the scene, but everything that wasn't burned down is visible in the remains.

Stepping over the tape with one leg, Richard places his skates on the debris to see if it is safe. Thankfully, my skates aren't rolling or getting debris stuck to them. Feeling good, he steps his other foot over as the others are already digging through the remains. Xena and Lowell mess around with each other as Christopher gets hands-on with the debris in silence.

Even though he wears business casual clothes and tuxedos, he doesn't mind getting a little dirty.

"*Are we looking for anything in particular?*" Christopher asks.

"*Not really. Just anything that stands out,*" Richard shrugs.

After he says that, something glistens in the corner of his eye, so he walks over to it.

Pushing burnt wood and metal pieces out of the way seeing something familiar in the item. It is a keychain with the number five on it. Seemed to be crafted by the same person who created the necklace Lowell got and the other numbered jewelry they all have.

"*Guys, I found a keychain with the number five on it. Similar design as the necklace Lowell got yesterday,*" Richard exclaims.

After he says that they all start talking interchangeably amongst each other, bouncing ideas off as if they are back to playing Lowell's treasure hunting game of death.

"*So, we are just skipping the number four now.*"

"*Maybe we will find the four later, Xena. Besides what if we are adding a fifth person to our group!?*" Christopher smiles at Xena.

"*I highly doubt that we are adding another person to this group,*" Richard replies.

"*Why don't we try finding out if Christopher's anklet, my necklace, and the keychain were manufactured by the same company? Once we know that, we can go to the company and look at their records over the past 50 years or so,*" Lowell adds in.

"*Well, we might as well add in the ring I got with the number two on it,*" Richard shrugs, showing them his ring.

Ever since his game when he was 15, he has worn this ring on and off because he found it on his room floor. He thought it was a birthday gift from his family.

It wasn't.

A raindrop lands on Xena's head. Then starts slowly coming down catching the group's attention. Looking up, they see dark grey clouds and lightning shoot across the sky. No thunder. Once we step across the caution tape, it starts pouring.

Lightning dashes across the sky every second they spend on the other side of the caution tape. No thunder.

A bolt of lightening lands two feet away from Lowell's foot and she screams. Another flash of lightening lands close as fear courses through all of their bodies.

Christopher scans the surroundings and yells at them to head towards the house. Lightning strikes the ground following them as if hunting them until they make it to the neighbors' porch. Breathing sharply, they all try to gather themselves as Xena frantically knocks on the door hopeful someone will open up.

Thunder rumbles loudly shaking the porch.

The door cracks slowly. The house looks dark. A young woman no older then Christopher, with golden brown eyes, looks through the door not undoing the chain. She has short pure white hair and it's noticeable through the cut that she has a baby wrapped against her chest.

"Can I help you?"

Richard and Lowell come forward and explain the situation how they are looking for shelter until the rain passes. Christopher investigates the distance before turning towards the woman. The baby on her chest leans back and stares into Xena's dark brown eyes with his brown eyes and jet-black hair.

"Just for a short while, I promise we aren't trying to be a bother," Lowell adds.

"I don't feel comfortable especially with my baby, we-"

Christopher turns around and she closes the door. They hear the chains unlocked and she slowly opens the door so they can fully see her. She looks like a goddess.

Tears fill her eyes.

"Christopher, darling, you're back?"

"Ophelia?"

THE HOLLOW REALM: AFTER THE SUMMONING

The sun rose outside a few moments ago. Sounds of no other souls have stepped foot out of their room yet. But in a home like this, one would wait till the first nightfall to start moving around.

I float towards Zilla's door, opening it fast.

Walking in yelling, "I've gone through all the events, I don't understand how-"

I pause.

She looks over at me as I see Ubel lying in the bed next to her. He stares at me and then gets up to exit, but Zilla grabs his hand to stay. Swallowing my anger, I look over at her. She looks in my direction but seems too distracted to make eye contact. All her other senses, hearing, taste, touch, and smell, are "overpowered," so I know she can feel when we are making eye contact. Besides, she can feel my energy like that.

"Did I hinder something?" I say in a cold tone.

"I could come back later."

"No, no, I think it's time for me to leave anyway. We're done here," Ubel signs, climbing through the vent in the roof of her room quickly.

I swear he never uses a door.

"What were you going to say, Pandora?" Zilla asks as he closes the vent.

"Nothing. I was just going to say that I didn't understand why I almost killed your human when I was summoned by mine a few hours ago…but it doesn't matter now."

She frowns, glancing down at her bedsheets.

"Ubel and I weren't taking part in any sneaky actions. We were just conversing about the humans, okay?"

"And if you were sneaking, that'd be fine," I say in my raspy tone, turning around to exit.

She magically teleports in front of me.

"What do you mean by 'that'd be fine?' You sound angered."

"So what if I am?" I say sliding by her, so I can leave.

She teleports in front of the door. And blocks me. It takes everything inside of me to not disappear into thin air right now. Sizing me up and down, she then touches the side of my face. The soft warm feel causes me to stop floating and place my feet onto the ground.

"Why are you mad, dear? There are five of us here and only one is you. I wouldn't risk our soul connection for a friend that can't stay in a room for more than a few seconds?" she says, looking into my eyes.

Her heart races fast, just like when we met each other for the first time all those years ago.

"You're right."

I glance at the fingers on my left hand.

"Perhaps I'm just missing you and upset that he was the first to lay eyes on you after the sun rose."

I'm missing my wedding ring. Better find it soon before Zilla finds out or decides to hold my hand. She'll probably beat me up if she finds out that I misplaced it during our expedition into the woods yesterday.

She smiles, tilting my head down at her, bringing our lips closer.

"Is there something you would like to say to me about your whereabouts during yesterday's second nightfall?" She smiles.

Her soft hands caressing my chin. The other slowly makes its way around the frame of my body. My body starts to tingle a little.

"Well, my human summoned me, and your human was just so-" I sigh as Zilla moves her hand onto my neck, softly.

"I tried to kill her b-mmm-because she pulled a knife on me when I pushed my human to the side."

"Yeah, my human is a fighter. I almost wanted to kill her after she kicked me," she whispers.

Locking her eyes on my still upset expression.

"Though I assume you are bothered because you summoned me by accident yesterday? I just watched. Instead of coming out and interfering."

"My apologies, dear."

I reach my finger out and rub my nail under her grey eyes. Faintly smiling.

"I saw you. But that didn't bother me, it just made me not kill her. You need her."

She smiles and looks to the right.

I sigh, saddened.

"Yes, but I need you more. Just in a different way. You know my heart shall always belong to you regardless of this freedom plan my brother has been conjuring up for years."

"Likewise for mine. I'm just protective after what happened to you 8 full moons ago."

"I respect that."

She then rubs her hand through my long hair. Zilla lets out a cute smile, causing me to float in the air a little bit. I grab her waist and place my lips onto hers. Lifting her.

Her legs wrap around me, as I pin her back to the wall. We float off the ground, kissing each other passionately. My hands finding their way up her blouse, to her back. Everything about her body is so soft. Leaves me craving to be close even when we reach our climaxes.

As we cuddle in bed, the alarm goes off. Zilla sleeps through the faint ringing that is heard through every room in the place. As a group, we ignore the blue lights that flicker - they don't mean anything right now. It's more of a start to something. Either good or bad.

After five minutes, the alarm goes off. I see a small flash of red from under the door, but it disappears so quick that I feel like I'm seeing things. I feel the floor slightly vibrating under my bed.

Frilo then walks into the room.

"There is something wrong."

"What?" I yawn, then cock my head to the side.

"We are under attack but…"

"Only the blue light came on?"

"No, there was red too. They are trying to break through the outer wall."

I laugh.

"Who told you this?"

He steps forward to leave the room, looking back one more time. Zilla is now looking over in his direction.

"Pandora?"

"Yes?"

"Lock the door when I leave. Only take the vents to exit and get around."

He's serious.

"Where's Ubel?"

"In the vent above my room."

We feel a stronger vibration against the floor. Under Zilla's room door, we can see the middle room flicking red.

"Shit."

- FOR THOSE WHO ARE LOST. THIS WILL FIND YOU…

- VG

www.ingramcontent.com/pod-product-compliance
Lightning Source LLC
LaVergne TN
LVHW090609110826
845146LV00001B/310

* 9 7 9 8 2 1 8 4 2 6 3 8 5 *